In Search
of
Christian Leadership Character

Volume 1

In Search
of
Christian Leadership Character

Volume 1

John Zechariah

2014

In Search of Christian Leadership Character - Volume I — published by the Rev. Dr. Ashish Amos of the Indian Society for Promoting Christian Knowledge (ISPCK), Post Box 1585, Kashmere Gate, Delhi-110006.

ISBN: 978-81-8465-458-5

Laser typeset by

ISPCK, Post Box 1585, 1654, Madarsa Road, Kashmere Gate, Delhi-110006 • *Tel:* 23866323

e-mail: ashish@ispck.org.in • ella@ispck.org.in
website: www.ispck.org.in

Printed at Repro Knowledgecast Limited, Thane

Dedicated
to
Asian Academy for Leadership and Peace

Contents

viii CONTENTS

Preface

Around the world the church is growing at an extraordinary speed. This growth has brought great challenges. The greatest challenge is lack of quality and committed leadership. The church needs men and women who are more than just managers of people, money and organizations. Leadership is always crucial to the church and worldwide. At the present moment, there is an urgency of good leadership. We live at a time of first class problems and second class leadership. In pursuit of growth and prosperity, we have lost the biblical principles in selecting, training and encouraging right leaders for the church and its organization. Throughout the Bible we see God was looking for leaders, to achieve His purpose.

A Christian leader is one who inspires others to live in a Christ-like manner and lives with integrity. A Christian leader not only who directs another to believe in the teachings of Jesus Christ, but also sets an example and inspires others.

Christian leaders are supposed to be more than just a leader, but take a central role in taking people further, into God's plan and purpose and also encouraging others into a deeper relationship and understanding of God. A Christian leader needs to nurture great character and qualities such as sense of mission, high character and judgment and physical energy. If leaders are invited by God, they will have characteristics like- trust worthy, conviction, competence and charisma. Godly leaders will have fruits of spirit like love, joy, peace, longsuffering, kindness, faithfulness, gentleness and self-control.

The Bible consists hundreds of names in the Old and New Testament, who had great personalities with great leadership qualities and character, Abraham, Moses, Joshua, David, Nehemiah, Solomon etc. are a few examples.

Leadership and management are interrelated in an organization, or church or in a team. An organization or church is as good as its leader. Therefore, the good qualities and characteristics of a leader shape the performance and future of any organization. Most importantly a leader needs to be honest, hardworking, set an example to his/her team, display integrity and fairness, delegate responsibilities judiciously to his subordinates. A leader should have the ability to motivate and keep the morale of the team always at the peak. Leadership is not wielding authority – it is empowering people.

Many Christian leaders are looking for direction and sources. Leading God's people requires wisdom and a variety of skills. Sometime leaders look for direction in a wrong place. On many occasions I look for the information on leadership, it is often not easy to find in one book or two. Therefore, I felt that there is need for common laymen, church leaders, pastors and youth, a book that will provide easy access for Christian leadership from a different perspective.

I don't claim that this book – In Search of Christian Leadership-Character, is unique but I tried to deal with important aspects of Christian leadership in four volumes. The present volume will deal with characteristics of Christian leadership. This book consists of many author's ideas, but looked and analyzed, through my life experience as a Chairman of Association of Christian Institute of Social Concern in Asia and Asian Academy for Leadership and Peace.

The purpose of this book firstly, is to assist all those who wish to understand Christian leaderships from the perspective of character, in a simple language. Secondly, deal with the Christian leadership characteristics by providing biblical leaders examples and lots of reference material. Thirdly, use this book as a resource material for the laity, pastors and participants of various leadership training, seminars and workshops. Asian Academy for Leadership and Peace is already using it as a curriculum for leadership training.

I suppose, I haven't told you anything you didn't already know. But I do hope that this book will sharpen your thoughts, ideas, skills and abilities. Often readers may ask, what is the point in reading another book on leadership? I feel one should get maximum resources to become a great leader, hope this will give lot of it. I strongly believe, this book will answer many questions relating to leadership characteristics of a Christian leader.

Beyond mere formality or courtesy, I would like to record my thanks for my friends and colleagues for their support and encouragement. This book is an outcome of the encouragement, I received as a chairman of Asian Academy for Leadership and Peace, while I organized many seminars/workshops/trainings nationally and internationally.

John Zechariah

PART 1

Chapter 1

Introduction[1]

Being a leader is an important job, although it is not easy. The world needs – men and women who are more than just managers of people, money and organizations. Leadership is always crucial to the church and worldwide. But at the present moment, it seems to me good leadership is essentially urgent. It seems we live at a time of first class problems and second class leadership.

> *"Our leaders appear as exceptional... not for their greatness but their pettiness, nor for their capacity to inspire the nation but for their capacity to depress it"*
> (Peregrine Worsthrone)

Around the world, the generation of post-World War II, including Christian leaders has begun and led outstanding movements of evangelism, missions, education, lay ministries and social concern. Now many of these leaders will need to pass on the mantle to the younger generation. The present leaders must harness the energies of younger men and women to lead and develop churches and organizations.

Real leaders are in short supply. Every leader today should ask:

- *Who is going to take my place?*
- *Whom is God raising to take my place?*
- *How can I help and encourage new leadership?*

In pursuit of growth and prosperity, we have lost the biblical principles in selecting, training and encouraging right leaders for the church and its organizations. Throughout the Bible we see God was looking for leaders. God invites leaders to participate in leading people to achieve His purpose. God made it clear from the beginning. God's call is always consistent. *He said "have dominion"* (Genesis 1:28).

Then God said

> "Let us make man in our image, in our likeness, and let them rule over the fish of the sea and the birds of the air, over the livestock, over all the earth, and over all the creatures that move along the ground." (Genesis 1:26)

> "The Lord has sought out a man after his own heart and appointed him leaders of his people" (1 Samuel 12:14)

> "Go up and down the streets of Jerusalem, look around and consider, search through her squares. If you can find but one person who deals honestly and seeks the truth, I will forgive this city" (Jeremiah 5:1).

> "I look for a man among them who would build up the wall" (Ezekiel 22:30).

If leaders are invited by God they will have characteristics like – trust worthiness , conviction, competence and charisma. Godly leaders will have fruits of spirit.

> "……..the fruit of the Spirit is love, joy, peace, longsuffering, kindness, goodness, faithfulness, gentleness, self-control. Against such there is no law" (Galatians 5; 22-23).

When Moses came down from Mount Sinai, with the two tablets of the Testimony in his hands, he was not aware that his face was radiant because he had spoken with the LORD. When Aaron and all the Israelites saw Moses, his face was radiant, and they were afraid to come near him (Exodus 34:29-32).

Whenever God has a message, he looks for a messenger, who has obedient character, ability and desire to listen to God's call sincerely and efficiently, like Isaiah. (Isaiah 6:1-8)

God chooses leaders not based on titles, but faithfulness to the purpose. When the Israelites planned to conquer Jericho, they chose Rahab, a prostitute because she was wise, clever and courageous and very well knew God's purpose. Later she was blessed. (Joshua 6:17)

Are leaders born or made? One can learn and practice leadership qualities even if our skills are old and not dynamic. Some may not have natural leadership skills, but can learn and practice. A great Christian leader will have natural as well as spiritual skills. J. Oswald Sanders[*2] has shown the differences between natural and spiritual qualities:

Natural	**Spiritual**
Self-confident	*Confident in God*
Knows men	*Also knows God*
Makes own decisions	*Seeks God's will*
Ambitious	*Humble*
Creates methods	*Follows God's example*
Enjoys Command	*Delights in Obedience to God*
Seeks personal reward	*Loves God and others*
Independent	*Depends on God*

God chose Noah not because of skills, talents or social standing but because he was a righteous leader with faith in God. God knows how, whom and when He can choose a leader for His purpose. Noah found the grace in the eyes of God and took the lead to save the human race from extinction. So the Lord said,

> "I will wipe mankind, whom I have created, from the face of the earth--men and animals, and creatures that move along the ground

and birds of the air--for I am grieved that I have made them." But Noah found favor in the eyes of the LORD. (Genesis 6:7-8)

When God wants to do great things, He looks for a leader. Behind every great institution, there is a single leader, whose character determines the character of the organization he leads. The Methodist church would not have been there without John Wesley, the Salvation Army without William Booth and modern missionary without William Carey.

Leaders who focus only on increasing knowledge and skills will not be prepared for fulfilling life with value; they need to cultivate a good and noble character.

Leadership is not wielding authority,
It is empowering people.

Chapter 2

What is Leadership?

Before we start dealing with leadership, it is imperative to understand and grasp the meaning of leadership.

Who is a leader? According to the Webster on-line dictionary a leader is one who directs on a course of action or in a direction.

Leadership means a process of influencing people to accomplish a task or goal. Every organization has long and short term goals; a leader has to accomplish his/her task of achieving these goals with a team. Today, most leaders wish to work with a team rather than making a team to work to his/her wishes.

In a non-technical language, a leader is someone who has the courage to lead and the humility to help others lead.

A leader raises people's aspiration and encourages using energies to achieve their goals.

Leadership is not just a position but it is also action. Leadership is a process of getting things done through people. Good leadership works by working through people. Leaders see farther than others in the team, they also see quickly and clearly. They know better what to do? How to do? What will happen or anticipate the consequences of their actions? Greater the challenge, the greater is the need, for a great leader. Developing leaders in an organization is most essential. For all this good, efficient and effective leadership counts.

> Leadership is not wielding authority-
> it's empowering people
>
> Becky Brodin

Leadership is not a science. So being a leader is an adventure, because you can never know whether you will reach the goal aspired. Leadership is more art than science. The principles of leadership are constant but the application changes with every leader and every situation.[1]

Let me summarise the meaning of leadership based on D. Quinn Mills[2]

1. It is a process by which one person influences the thoughts, attitudes, and behaviors of others.

2. Leaders set a direction for the rest of us, they help us see what lies ahead, they help us visualize what we might achieve, and they encourage us and inspire us.

3. Leadership is the ability to get other people to do something significant that they might not otherwise do.

4. Leadership energizes people towards a goal

Leadership means responsibility. Both go together. One cannot separate leadership from relationship. From Paul's life and teaching leaders can learn:[3]

-   Avoid hypocrisy
-   Be loyal to colleagues

- Give preference to others
- Be hospitable
- Return good for evil
- Identify with others
- Be open – minded toward others
- Treat everyone with respect
- Do everything possible to keep peace
- Remove revenge from your life

A leader is a dealer in hope

The key to leadership is to accept responsibility

Leaders must follow, before they can lead

To be a leader you have to be at once with the people you can lead

Good followers don't make good leaders

Leaders must be ready to make hard decisions.

Leaders set high standards and inspire others to achieve

Effective leadership is the backbone of any organization including church. It allows utilizing organizations resources more efficiently. Able leadership will bring positive attitude among employees, which reflects an organizations performance. Lack of able leadership can bring negativity which will result in poor performance.

The English language has several synonyms for word "Leader". These different names reveal the different kinds of leaders that exist in the world. Leaders are called Shepherds, Rulers, Judges, Prophet, Commanders, Pastors, Captains, Honorable Citizens and Counselors. (Peter Nsowah).

A Christian leader is one who follows Christ and inspires others to follow him as well.

Chapter 3

Who is a Christian Leader?

According to the Webster on-line dictionary a Christian is one who professes and believes in the teachings of Jesus Christ.

The Greek word for "Christian," is *Christianos*. This means "follower of Christ; Christian."

The designation of the early followers of Christ as Christians was initiated by someone from another faith, and originally it was probably a term of mocking – "little Christ." Eventually, however, Christians used it of themselves as a name of honor, not of shame. Prior to their adoption of the name, the Christians called themselves believers, brothers or saints, names which also continued to be used..."[1]

If you take the above definitions and combine them, you get "One who directs another to believe in the teachings of Jesus Christ". But is this the true definition of a Christian leader? Leadership in anything that requires dedication, education, and desire/passion. Therefore, to be a Christian leader is to dedicate your life to the savior, educate yourself on your savior, and desire to follow God's will. By that definition it seems to me, anyone who loves the Lord can be a Christian leader. A Christian leader is one who inspires others to live in a Christ-like manner and lives with integrity. A

Christian leader is not only "One who directs another to believe in the teachings of Jesus Christ" but also sets an example and inspires others to live as we do. A Christian leader helps others in need, shows passion and love for the Lord,

> *You must live with people to know their problems, and live with God in order to solve them.*
>
> **P. T. Forsyth**

and is humble in all things. A Christian leader does not have to be a pastor, deacon, or elder of the church, look right next to you and you may see a dedicated choir member, an ambitious young adult, or a child memorizing a Bible verse, and these are the Christian Leaders. Just by being a Christian you are already a leader.

Michael Houdmann[2] describes – what is Christian leadership?

1. He is one who acts as a shepherd to those "sheep" in his/ her care.

2. A Christian leader is one who follows Christ and inspires others to follow Him as well.

3. A Christian leader nourishes his/her flock with food, which will produce strong, vibrant Christians.

4. As Christians in the world today, we suffer from many injuries spiritually and we need compassionate leaders who will bear our burdens with us, sympathize with our circumstances, exhibit patience toward us, encourage us in the word, and bring our concerns before the Father's throne.

5. A Christian leader corrects and disciplines those in his or her care when they go astray.

6. The Lord disciplines those he loves, and a Christian leader must follow his or her example.

7. The final role of a Christian leader is that of a protector.

Many of us believe, leaders are naturally gifted with intellect, professional efficiency and enthusiasm These qualities definitely improve leadership potential, but they cannot be spiritual leaders, unless they are willing to sacrifice and suffer for a greater mission and vision wholeheartedly. There are certain godly principles to note: we must rise up, we must pursue, we must recover all, don't lie down and give up, don't run and don't stick your head in the sand[3].

John MacArthur[4] explained in his article "wanted": A few Good Shepherds.

"Under the plan God has ordained for the church, leadership is a position of humble, loving service. Church leadership is ministry, not management. Those whom God designates as leaders are called not to be governing monarchs, but humble slaves; not slick celebrities, but laboring servants. Those who would lead God's people must above all exemplify sacrifice, devotion, submission, and lowliness. Jesus Himself gave us the pattern when He stooped to wash His disciple's feet, a task that was customarily done by the lowest of slaves. If the Lord of the universe would do that, no church leader has a right to think of himself as bigwig."

Leadership is an opportunity,
one needs to grab and hold it for the future.

Chapter 4

Importance of Leadership

Leadership is important in every human activity in history. Good leadership helps nations through times of peril, it makes business organization or church successful, enables NGO's to fulfill its vision and mission, enables children to grow and become productive adults. On the other hand, lack of good leadership can bring negative results. People don't want managers but leaders. An American said for Jimmy Carter, the then president of United States of America, "You are managing a nation Mr. President, but you are not giving us leadership."

During 1930 most English men refused to follow Winston Churchill, when he reminded threat from Hitler's Germany. They rejected his leadership and Churchill had very few followers. When Germany went too far and war began, Churchill's foresight became true. Then Churchill's leadership was recognized and accepted as Prime Minister of United Kingdom. Churchill became a real and great leader. In leadership rejections are common, but never give up till you reach success. Leaders can do less but achieve more.

Leadership skills, talents can be perverted to pursue bad intentions like Hitler. Hitler had great skills of a leader, but he set an evil

> "If your actions inspire others to dream more, learn more, do more and become more, you are a leader"
> (John Quincy)

direction. At times in an organization or church or NGO leadership skills are used to exploit the organization. Therefore, ethical values play an important role in the life a leader. As per D. Quinn Mills taking leadership means:

- *Having a vision about what can he accomplished*
- *Making commitment to the mission and to the people you lead*
- *Taking responsibility for the accomplishment of the mission and the welfare of those you lead*
- *Assuming risk of loss and failure*
- *Accepting recognition for success*

To be a leader is far more important than just to be a good human being . Leadership is the ability to make goodness operate in the lives of others. Everything rises and falls on leadership, therefore never underestimate the importance of leadership. When a strong leader with values at the helm of the church/organization, such church/organization is flourishing, their members are developing and achieve breakthrough after breakthrough. We see on other hand few churches/ organization are failing, the problem is the leader and not anything else.

Leadership is a journey filled with exciting moments, days of victories and days of defeats. Bill Cosby says *"I don't know the key to success, but the key to failure is trying to please everybody"*. A successful journey takes time and commitment to become effective leadership. Being a leader is a commitment to growth and the willingness to bear the responsibilities that come with leadership journey.

History is crafted by men and women of influence. Leaders have created histories. Wars have been caused by one leader with ambition, like horrifying stories of Adolf Hitler, who wanted to make Germans the strongest race on earth. Mother Teresa, created history of love, compassion and care, she chose to bring a positive change and difference. Mahatma Gandhi is the one who changed the history, by gaining India's independence without violence. Abraham Lincoln, the one leader who could abolish slavery. The 21st century needs more and more leaders with positive, strong and firm values.

Every Christian is a leader who has to fulfill his/her leadership destiny.

> "What no one ever saw or heard what no one ever thought could happen, is the very thing God prepared for those who love him" (1 Corinthians 2:9).

Leadership is an opportunity, one needs to grab and hold it for the future.

> "I alone know the plans I have for you plan to bring you prosperity and not disaster, plans to bring about the future your hope for" (Jeremiah 29:11).

Christian leadership starts with the conception of vision. Moses acknowledged as one of the great leaders of all time. When did he become a leader? Scholars believe that he became a leader when he confronted Pharaoh. Jesus is certainly the greatest leaders of all times. His leadership started the movement he left heaven with the vision of giving his own life for our sins. Abraham, who is known as father of faith, gives us the very first example of Christian leadership. He received vision from God and acted on it by believing in God.

It is not easy to become a successful leader, unless you know what people expect from you. John. Maxwell, [2] highlights the need of leader:

> "Family and friends need leader, who model purpose – driven life
>
> Children need leaders who help them reach their potential
>
> Churches need leaders' who chart the course and equip the saints

Business need leaders who build great places to work while making a profit

Communities need leaders who create a better place to live"

People go to universities and spend 5 to 6 years to become doctors or engineers, but unfortunately no preparation or training, seems necessary for leadership, while these leaders will lead and will have authority over the society. It is therefore, necessary that schools, colleges and universities take a lead to train leaders. We at Asian Academy for Leadership and Peace (AALP), give training of leadership to various segments of society.

I feel it is worth mentioning 10 steps for leadership Chairman Azim Premji[3] of Wipro Corporation,

- Leaders must develop powerful personal credibility
- Great leaders tell people clearly what they expect from them
- Great leaders are great teachers
- Successful leaders need to have energy and be able to energize others
- Leaders do not always have to be the limelight
- Winning leaders face reality
- Leaders keep renewing themselves
- Leaders surround themselves with people who err on the side of optimism
- Leaders play to win
- Leaders respect themselves (confidence)

From management point of view leadership is an important function, which helps to maximize efficiency and to achieve organizational goal, which is true with Christian leaders. One can justify how important leadership in action, in management and churches today[4] initiates action

1. Motivation

2. Providing guidance

3. Creating confidence

4. Building morale

5. Builds work environment

6. Co-ordination

Leadership plays an effective role in accomplishing the set objectives, with his/her team taking into consideration the strengths and weakness of human resources and utilizes them efficiently for maximum success. Motivation role of a leader is crucial for success. A leader will also create a harmonious environment, for maximum advantage.

.....men are primarily task-oriented but women tend to be both, task-and relationship-oriented.

Chapter 5

Types of Leadership

A leadership style is a leader's style of providing direction, implementing plans and motivating people. Different situations call for different leadership styles. The style adopted should be the one that most effectively achieves organizational goals, taking into consideration the interest of the member of an organization.

There is a vast difference in the various leadership styles. These are basic yet effective styles which help us understand the concept clearly.

The way a leader leads is important. There are nine broad *"styles"* of leadership:

1. Autocratic Leadership

Autocratic, the leader has complete authority and control. The autocratic styles are old and commonly used in earlier times. This is the military type of style with a touch of dictatorship. In this style, the work of the leader is to make others follow the rules. This method is effective in certain situations; that need a stern hand but the disadvantages are far too many like, low morale of the workers, rebellion of followers etc.

2. Democratic Leadership

In a democratic style the entire group shares in decision making. This style encourages team work, where a team comes for a collective decision. In this type, everyone's opinions are taken into consideration. The disadvantages caused by the above method are ruled out in this style. This style is also known as participative leadership style.

3. Laissex-Faire Leadership

In Laissez-faire-the leader exerts little influence or control. A French term, which means "let it be". In this style a leader leaves the individuals to complete the tasks. The leader leaves goal setting and target setting in the hands of the individuals itself. This style involves minimum interference from the leader and much freedom for the followers. On the downside, many tend to take advantage of this form of leadership.

4. Result-Centered Leadership

In this style of functioning, achievement is the goal and in itself involves the motivation of the workers. The worker is tailored to provide the greatest motivation for the workers.

5. Situational Leadership

A leader is required to balance the following factors:

A. The extent of rapport or good feeling between the leader and the followers.

B. The nature of the job to be done in terms of specification and procedures.

C. The amount of real power invested in the leader.

6. Theocratic Leadership

This is only true and acceptable Christian leadership style. God is in charge and the Christian leaders obey His directives. God provides the vision, the strategy and the resources[1] (Number 4-6, as mentioned in article Gladiators for God).

7. Narcissistic Leadership

Narcissistic leadership is a style in which the leader is only interested in himself or herself , at the expense of his/her organization and people. Here the leaders exhibit characteristics of arrogance, dominance and hostility.

8. Toxic Leadership

A toxic leader is someone who has responsibility over a group of people and who abuses the leader-follower relationship by leaving the group or organization in a worse-off condition than when he or she joined it.

9. Sex Difference in Leadership Behavior

When men and women come together in group, they tend to adopt different leadership styles. Men generally assume dominating leadership style. They are task-oriented, decision focused, independent and goal oriented. On the other hand, women are generally more communal when they assume a leadership position, they strive to be helpful towards others, warm in relations to others, understanding, and mindful of others feelings. They often give advice, offer assurances and manage conflicts in an attempt to maintain positive relationships among group members. Women connect more positively to groups by smiling, maintaining eye contact and respond tactfully to other comments. Men on the other hand are influential, powerful and proficient and task oriented.

As leaders, men are primarily task-oriented but women tend to be both task-and relationship-oriented.[2]

"There are also different levels of leadership. There is leadership based on great causes; pragmatic leadership; leadership emanating from the barrel of gun; leadership based on principles and finally that rare level of transforming leadership."[3]

Dr. Stephen L. Cohen[4] mentions fourth leadership practices – "Engaging Style" for leading organization in tough times. The initiatives demands engaging leaders and employees in understanding the existing conditions and how they can collectively assist to overcome. Reaching employees means; to understand their concerns and interests openly and honestly.

Christian leaders need to have a servant heart.

Chapter 6

Principles of
Christian Leadership

Leadership means leading people and influencing them. John Maxwell believes, Christian leaders are supposed to be more than this. Christian leaders are people who are moved at God's pace and in God's time to God's place. Christian leadership is about taking a central role in taking people further into God's plans and purposes and encouraging others into a deeper relationship and understanding of God.

The foundation of Christian leadership is to have intimate relations with God, through prayer and Bible studies; this will help to see the world from God's eyes, with servant heart and attitude of shepherd. Of course attitude of integrity and humility are important.

Remember the principles of good Christian leadership[1]

- Christian leadership should manifest deep personal conviction
- Christian leadership should maintain rigorous personal schedules
- Christian leadership should place all their lives in subordination to their goals

- Christian leadership should be willing to make hard decision
- Christian leadership should learn to live with tension

A Christian leader needs to nurture great qualities such as, a sense of mission, high character, good judgment and physical energy.

If you desire to be Christian leader in the true sense of the word, I would like to suggest that you better say the following prayer, which was first prayed by General Douglas McArthur[2] for his son:

> "Build me, Oh Lord, to be strong enough to know when I am weak and brave enough to face myself when I am afraid, let be proud and unbending in honest, defeat and humble and gentile in victory.

> "Build me to be a person whose wishes will not take the places of deeds; let me know Thee... and help me realize that to know myself is the foundation stone of knowledge".

> Build me to be a person whose heart will be clear, whose goal will be high, a person who will master himself before he seeks to master other men; one who will reach into the future, yet never forget the past"

> "And after all these things are mine, add, I pray, enough of a sense of humor, so that may always be serious, yet never take myself too seriously"

> "Give me humility so that I may remember the simplicity of true generation, the open mind of true wisdom and the meekness of true strength. Then I, will dare to whisper, I have not lived in vain" Amen.

One of the greatest principles of Christian leadership is credibility even during crisis. A leader has to be a good model for his followers. Paul while dealing with Corinthian church, asked people to do something he had not already done. Paul sacrificed life. Every leader can learn from Paul's life as a good model leader, as mentioned by[3]

- *His leadership was on display and open for ridicule*
- *He was willing to play the fool in order to model a surrendered life*
- *He endured mocking from others, but didn't waver*
- *He sacrificed luxuries that others enjoyed*

- *He urged his followers to imitate his life*
- *He sent Timothy to help them live up to godly standards*
- *He remodeled them that God's kingdom was not about talk, but power.*

Leadership is caught more than taught.

Leaders must set an example for their followers as Moses. People do what they see. People watched Moses as he spent time with God, interceding for them in intimate, personal communion - and it changed them more than any sermon could have.[4]

Why is God the greatest leader and can be the best model? It is because – everything around us changes but God's promises never changes, God's promises never fail, God's promises always prevail and you will get encouragement, comfort and inspiration to face challenges with God's promises.

The success of a true and competent leader depends- when he or she perceives a need or spots a specific problem, possess a gift; has the competence to address the need, parades passion; casts vision for a passion to act, persuades people; attracts others to join the cause, pursues a purpose; employs measures to accomplish the desired goal[5].

As John Maxwell believes Christian leaders have extra responsibilities or principles to follow:

Dave Quinn[6] suggests five principles vital to a Christian leader to follow:

- Christian leaders need to cultivate an intimate relationship with God
- Christian leaders need to have a servant heart

- Christian leaders need to be shepherds of God's people
- Christian leaders need to live with character and integrity
- Christian leaders need to be committed to making disciples

The moment you stop learning, you stop leading

Chapter 7

Christian Leadership Formation[1]

L eadership formation is an understanding what leadership is and the configuring or shaping it to fit the definition of leaders. It involves helping people identify and develop the sources within themselves. Leadership formation means leadership development which includes spiritual and administrative formation or development. Leaders need to be encouraged to develop their own spiritual and administrative abilities for organization. They should engage faithfully and regularly in their prayerful life and also with the organizations and churches they belong to.

Leadership Development Plan[2]

Leadership development plan has to include the goals you plan to achieve as a leader. Each leader has to create personal leadership development plan based on vision and goals. This will enable him/ her not only to be a manager, but more important to become a good leader.

Dwight Eisenhower said "Leadership is the art of getting someone else to do something you want done because he wants to do it" He underlines importance of picking "right people to do the right job" and the important job of a leader to be a motivator.

To become a true leader demands self-introspection, planning and execution.

Every action is important but it should be guided by vision and plan. Personal leadership plan is essential for organizational plan. Leader's strengths, weakness and vision are vital for any organization. A leader needs to be aware of opportunities and roadblock in his/her leadership. A leader has to bring best out of him/her and team. A great leader inspires his/her followers to reach higher levels of excellence. To be an effective leader, you need to have followers and they should allow you to be the leader and believe in you. The important part of leadership development plan is to improve your own performance and bring positive changes in the organization by setting an example.

Leadership development plan needs to be based on extensive introspection or assessment about one's leadership style and working culture of organization, its strengths and weakness.

Leadership is the ability of identifying and developing one's resources, human and materials, mobilizing those resources to realize one's vision, reach one's goals, and solve one's problems.

Teaching and learning are important tools in a leader's life. Therefore, leaders are lifelong learners. *The movement you stop learning, you stop leading* – Rick Warren. Christian leader has to follow the greatest model, Jesus Christ. This enables to practice qualities such as humility, courage, sharing, sacrifice, love, and ability to follow.

Leadership formation is challenging because it involves learning and education. Education is a key in leadership formation. Ira Shore[3] writes that there are eleven aspects to empowering education which are the keys to leadership formation. Namely, they are participative, effective, researching, interdisciplinary, situated, multicultural, activist, problem-posing, dialogic, de-socializing and democratic.

Each of us dream, mainly two dreams:

1. Are you willing to dream of doing great things?

2. Are you willing to set goals that will move you toward making that dream a reality?

If you wish to develop and explore your leadership abilities:

*   You not only **Dream Big**
*   You not only **Think Big**
*   You not only **Plan Big**
*   You **Act Big**

Lack of managerial skills or effective leadership is a serious problem in any organization. Some people have natural leadership gifts. Unfortunately, most don't fall in this category; therefore, we have to acquire leadership skills based on understanding of human behavior.

All of us can be leaders and the decision is up to us. A man has almost 80 billion brain cells of which he or she uses only a tenth (8 billion). There is unlimited potential within humans which can be tapped if he or she sets his/her mind to do so.

Nehemiah's leadership is not only an eye opener for Christian leadership but also a practical, reliable guideline, to be become a leader:

*   Balancing practical planning with trust in God
*   Coping with undeserved criticism
*   Resolving personality conflicts and strained human relationship
*   Facing financial crunch
*   Handling executive burnout

Christian leadership is defined as:

- Christian leadership seeks to the service, rather than to dominate
- Christian leadership encourages and inspires
- Christian leadership respects rather exploits other's personalities
- Christian leadership reflects, prays and acts on God's works

Characteristics of leadership, apart from being discipline, humble, honest, sincere, faithful, dynamic hard working, patience and understanding, Christian leadership should have following:

- Good attitude (example of Plato)
- Servant leadership or sense of call
- Enables others to experience that life in its fullness
- Concern/love and consider all human beings are most important resources that leader needs
- Self development, capacity, confidence and decisiveness
- Capability- intelligence, alertness, verbal facility, originality and judgment

  * Achievement – scholarship, knowledge and accomplishment
- Responsibility – dependability, initiative, persistence, aggressiveness, self-confidence and desire to excel
- Commitment.

"Every great institution is a lengthened shadow of a single man. His character determines the character of his organization" – Ralph Waido Emerson.

A good leader has to understand the *pre-requisites* for his or her leadership:

- Be willing to pay the price for what he or she wants
- Learn to accept responsibilities
- Learn to accept help from others
- Spend time on important issues
- Express your feeling and understand other's feeling
- Establish and maintain good relations with others
- Face problems in terms of the present, not the past or the future
- Appraise your own performance honestly
- Before attempting to manage others, manage yourself first
- Participation with activity, sociability, cooperation, adaptability and humor
- Initiative ability to be a self-starter
- Ability to gain respect and to win the confidence of others
- Ability to communicate through people at various levels
- Accomplishment with quantity and quality of work produced through effective use of time
- Flexibility includes ability to cope with change to adjust to the unexpected
- Objectivity includes ability to control personal feelings, open mindedness
- Basic knowledge and information such as command over basic facts, relevant professional knowledge.

"It is good to think well, it is divine to act well. A good leader acts" (Horace Mann).

Leaders always have to think what he can do? Watch your can's and cant's.

- You cannot aim low and then rise
- You cannot succeed if you don't try
- You cannot go wrong and come out right
- You cannot love sin and walk in light
- You cannot throw time and means away
- You cannot be great if you'll be good

Therefore, watch the way you talk and act and don't take the false for fact.

"So life is great to every man, who lives to do the best he can".

Leadership Behavior

Leadership behavior can be: 1. Leader - center 2. Group - center.

In leader center type leader use more authority and persuade the team members, while group center type leader provides freedom to the team by consulting, asking them to participate and finally he delegate's responsibilities.

Leadership is more of influence. In every leadership styles there are few factors that influence.

1. Personality of a Leader
   - Leader's value system
   - Leader's confidence in the group
   - Leader's inclination
2. Personality of the Group members
   - Their need for independence
   - Their desire for responsibility
   - Their skill, etc.

3. Nature of task
   * It's importance and complexity
   * Its urgency
4. Nature of the environment and structure of an organization.
   * Outside pressure: Social, economic and political

When faith is lost, when honor dies the man is dead.

Chapter 8

Basic Qualifications[1] of Christian Leader

Christian leadership should have *basic qualification* such as:

1. *Faith*: Faith is the most important qualification of a Christian leader. This is true with Moses, when he became sure of God and of the divine intention, the people followed him. Israelites tested his faith again and again and when it held fast against all odds, they followed him all the way to Canaan.

Faith will remove fears with the blessing of God. Moses encountered fear before his encounter with God. He placed himself before God. Moses dealt all kinds fears:

- Fears concerning himself

- Fears concerning God

- Fears concerning others

- Fears concerning his abilities

> **When faith is lost, when honors dies the man is dead**

A leader has to sacrifice his/her pride and self-reliance and prepare his/her life for the purpose for which God calls. If you wish to lead, you must be ready to make sacrifices. Leaders are required to encourage themselves in God standing firm in faith and say.

"Though He slay me yet will I trust Him (Job 13:15).

2. *Sensitive care of persons.* A caring person makes the best leader for the church. This was true with Moses experience. We also get some hint from Elijah's caring in the story of his tenderness towards widow and her son.

3. *A leader's authority.* Authority is a kind of power. Power is capability of making things happen in an organization; this means the ability to see that person acts in certain ways. If you wish to know what a wo/ man is, place her/him in authority. A leader needs to know that ultimately authority belongs to people. The boss depends upon authority the leader depends on good will. "Leadership is not wielding authority – it's empowering people" – Becky Brodin.

Authority creates order in an organization. Imagine a nation without a leader and authority. Respect those in authority over you. Your success depends on such authority. Learn to respect seniors and elders because they possess a wealth of knowledge. Listen, learn and observe them, you will be benefited.

Slaves, obey your earthly masters with respect and fear, and with sincerity of heart, just as you would obey Christ. Obey them not only to win their favor when their eye is on you, but like slaves of Christ, doing the will of God from your heart. (Ephesians 6:5-6).

Let us not forget that Jesus respected authority.

4. *Leader as a coordinator.* It involves among other things, developing the minds of the group's life together, securing their acceptance of this model keeping it up to date. "Coming together is a beginning, keeping together is progress and working together is success."

5. *Leader's faith in planning and people.* Planning process includes the classification of purpose, analysis of the project, identifying the problems, listing the possibilities and starting a project or program.

6. *Leader's structure* To carry out the plan, personnel arrangement, provision of resources, time frame and celebration.

Ryan C. Nielsen[2] mentions qualifications of a leader. The most important qualification of a Christian leader is passion for the Lord, Jesus Christ and compassion for all people. Further, s/he mentions:

1. A positive role model
2. A person of integrity
3. Ability to identify with the problems, needs and feelings of youth
4. Patient
5. Good listener
6. Positive attitude and good sense of humor
7. Willingness to give necessary time

A good leader always has to think what s/he can do and what he or she cannot. So watch:

1. You cannot aim low and then rise high.
2. You cannot succeed if you don't try.
3. You cannot go wrong and come out right.
4. You cannot throw time and means away.
5. You cannot be great if you like to be just good.

Life is great to every man, who lives to do the best he can.

Leadership behavior normally depends, whether leadership is leader centered or group centred. These behaviors include use of authority or freedom of the group. In leader-centered leadership, see more of order less of persuasion, consultation, participation and delegation of power and responsibilities with the group.

In any style or behavior of leadership, people will follow the leader depending on charisma, tradition and rationality. Charisma means the quality in a leader which makes people follow his or her orders. In Christian traditional leadership today, there is backing of a rich tradition, which gives legitimacy of his or her use of power. Leadership rationality of using power, style of function etc. are important.

Leaders need right kind of advisors who have qualities such as – fear of God, respect to the leader, people centric, and experience. King Saul died because he was unfaithful to the Lord and his advisors.

When King Rehoboam consulted the elders for advice, elders advised him to be kind to the people and please them and give them a favorable answer, they will be always be your servants. Out of his arrogance and on the advice of his younger friends, he rejected the advice of elders. When leaders rebuke leaders with knowledge and experience the consequence will be negative where people revolted against Rehoboam. (2 Chronicles 10:6).

Over Come Criticism

Leaders are more subject to criticism than any other people are. One of the costs of leadership is criticism. If you want to stand tall from the crowd as a leader, put yourself in vulnerable possible position, to count some degree of criticism. Here the question is not that "Will I be criticized?" but "How will I handle and learn from criticism? John Maxwell suggests few tips on criticisms.

a. Ask if there is any truth in the criticism. Is God saying something to you?

b. Don't take yourself too seriously.

c. Look beyond the criticism and see the critic.

d. Watch your own attitude toward the critic.

e. Keep physically and spiritually in shape.

f. Don't just see the critic, see if there is a crown.

g. Wait for time to prove them wrong.

h. Surround yourself with positive people.

i. Concentrate on your mission – change your mistakes.

Leadership is about vision that empowers.
Leadership is the capacity to translate vision into reality.

PART 2

Chapter 9

Characteristics of Leadership[1]

L eadership and management are interrelated in an organization or in a team. An organization or a team is as good as its leader. Therefore, eventually, the good qualities and characteristics of a leader shape the performance and future of organization. Most importantly a leader needs to be honest, hardworking, set an example to his or her team, display integrity and fairness, delegate responsibilities judiciously to his/her subordinates.

Only position doesn't make a leader. David was leading his people long before Saul had lost his throne. Then all Israel came together to David at Hebron, saying,

> 'Indeed we are your bone and your flesh. Also in time past, even when Saul was king, you were the one who led Israel out and brought them in; and the Lord your God said to you, "You shall shepherd My people Israel, and be ruler over My People Israel" (1 Chronicles 11:1-2).

Title may give someone authority, but not influence, influence has to be earned. David had earned it and Saul had not because, David rallied the people and created unity, he identified with his followers as a family, he effectively led military campaigns, he enjoyed God's hand and power on his life and he worked cooperatively with key leaders.[2]

A Christian leader is one who inspires others to live in a Christ-like manner and lives with integrity. A Christian leader not only "One who directs another to believe in the teachings of Jesus Christ" but also sets an example and inspires others to live as we do. A Christian leader helps others in need, shows his passion and love for the Lord, and is humble in all things.

Isaiah suggests following qualities for a leader to stand firm during the crisis and disappointment – integrity, justice, convictions, positive focus, pure and clean mind and stable in his identity and strength (Isaiah 33:14-16).

Leadership is all about knowing and understanding people to fulfill vision and mission. To understand the people and to get work done, a good leader will have characteristics like, vision, integrity, honesty, dedication and commitment, above self, skills and knowledge and courage not to accept the failure.

The way a leader leads is important. There are three broad *"styles"* of leadership:

1. *Autocratic* - the leader has complete authority and control
2. *check* - the entire group shares in decision making
3. *Laissez* - faire-the leader exerts little influence or control

We can describe leaders from several perspectives, each of which casts a different light on what goes into the complex task of leadership responsibilities. We need strong leaders of good character in all places, who will have character of integrity, dependability and righteousness.

A boss creates fear

A leader confidence

A boss fixes blame,

A leader corrects mistakes.

A boss knows all

A leader asks questions.

A boss makes work drudgery,

A leader makes it interesting.

A boss is interested in himself or herself,

A leader is interested in the group. (Russell H. Ewing)

Character means distinctive quality of a person, a strong personal quality, a person's good reputation. Character is the utmost of importance for anyone desiring to be in church leadership. Character is something which comes out of our lives not just something we put into our lives. Character is beyond a system of values or virtue we learn from our parents or church. Our parents and churches can teach character but they cannot put it into action, except us. The church leadership should always be guided by God's call.

"Character building begins in our infancy and continues to death"
"Leaders must live by higher standards than their follower"
(Anonymous)

Visionary

The leader has to be practical and a realist yet must talk the language of the visionary and the Idealist. Eric Hoffer

Vision means the ability to think about the future with imagination or wisdom. *Vision is the art of seeing things invisible* (Jonathan Swift). A visionary is one who thinks about the future with imagination and wisdom. Leadership is about vision that empowers. *Leadership is the capacity to translate vision into reality* (Warren G. Bennis). Leadership is the transference of vision. 'Leaders have visions that make a difference, empowering visions that offer hope for tomorrow and shape behaviors today'. *"Where there is no vision, the people perish"*. *The most pathetic person in the world is someone who has sight but has no vision* (Helen Keller). For a successful leader, just having vision is not enough but he or she should have a plan and ability to implement for successful end. A great leader follows his or her vision and strives for success, than wanting to get all the credit.

Many of the best leaders lead via vision. Such leaders get an idea that they want to share with others. The idea is often a mental picture of a possible future, based on biblical principles combined with imagination or possibly, an actual special revelatory "vision" from God. This idea excites such leaders or fills them with longing. They want others to see what they see and appreciate how cool it would be. A leader may not always develop a new unique vision, but may buy into another's vision. Some studies suggest that the best leaders are not necessarily the most creative people in a community, although they are usually more creative than average. Whether the leader's vision is original or borrowed is unimportant. Leaders need to have long-range vision to avoid short-run failures and discouragements. Good leaders practice ways to communicate their visions, tying future pictures to past realities, showing how such a picture is better than the status quo. They can explain why attaining such a vision justifies risk and pain. Followers of visionaries find their excitement contagious, and accept the leader's vision as their own. They find themselves highly motivated to attain the vision, usually without much consideration of personal benefit

A strong power of vision will motivate, keep leaders priorities straight, develop his/her potentials, and help him/her to evaluate his/her leadership. Paul's leadership is right example; even while he was in prison he kept his vision and purpose strong and straight.

Vision is everything for a leader. It is utterly indispensable because vision leads the leader. Vision paints, sparks and fuels the fire within, and draws them forward. It is also fire-lighter for others who follow those leaders. To get a handle on vision and how it comes to be a part of a good leader, understand these things: (John Maxwell)

- Vision starts within
- Vision draws on your history
- Vision meets others' needs
- Vision helps you gather resources

> "The very essence of leadership is that you have to have vision. You can't blow an uncertain trumpet"
>
> Theodore M. Hesburgh

One of the most valuable benefits of vision is that it acts like a magnet-attracting, challenging, and uniting people. The greater the vision, the more winners it has the potential to attract. The more challenging the vision, the harder the participants fight to achieve it.

All leaders have vision but not all people who possess vision are leaders. A compelling vision alone will not make someone a leader. Nor will a great vision automatically be fulfilled simply because it is compelling or valuable. Just because a person has vision and occupies a leadership, position does not necessarily mean that the people will follow. Before they follow the leader, they have to trust and have confidence on a leader. People need to know the leader's vision clearly, so that they can follow with confidence. John Maxwell says every vision message possesses – clarity, connectedness, purpose, goals, honesty, stories, challenge, passion, accountability to vision and strategy.

A bigger vision drives God's vision. God's blessings follow leaders who adopt His vision for the nations and the world. *Godly leaders feel driven to fulfill His visions.*

The value of vision is very crucial for a leader and organization. Therefore, value the vision. The great vision can be:

— Vision unites

— Vision provides a center for leadership

— Vision dominates inner voice or conversation

— Vision inspires greatness

— Vision attracts greatness

Vision brings victory. God's vision for Paul accomplished number of things: (John Maxwell)

- *It stopped him* – *Vision allows seeing ourselves. We see things not as they are, but as we are*

- *It sent him* – Vision allows us to others. We feel compelled to act

- *It strengthened him* – Vision enables us to continue despite struggles and lack of resources

- *It stretched him* – Vision gives us conviction to stand, confidence to speak, and compassion to share

- *It satisfied him* – Obedience to this vision motivates us to act.

The success of leadership depends not only on the organization's vision but also leader's and each member of the team. When the Spirit is poured on all flesh, men and women shall see visions and dreams.

Spiritual leaders must always give direction on vision and goals, to the followers by submitting their lives to God. Zechariah was a great visionary who risked his life to pass on God's message to people of Judah and Jerusalem. After the death of Jehoiada, the officials of Judah came and paid homage to the king, and he listened to them. They abandoned the temple of the Lord, the God of their fathers, and worshiped Asherah poles and idols. Because of their guilt, God's anger came upon Judah and Jerusalem. Although the Lord sent prophets to the people to bring them back to him, and though they testified against them, they would not listen. Then the spirit of the God came upon Zechariah son of Jehoiada the priest. He stood before the people and said,

> "This is what God says: 'Why do you disobey the Lord's commands? You will not prosper. Because you have forsaken the Lord, he has forsaken you'".

However, people plotted against him, and by the order of the king, they stoned him to death in the courtyard of the Lord's temple (2 Chronicles 24:17-22).

Leaders see both problem and solution, like Nehemiah who never visited Jerusalem. All great leaders have common vision. A leader sees farther than other see, more than other see, and before others see. Nehemiah had these qualities (Nehemiah 2:5).

Sometimes leader's vision has double meaning. Moses' vision for Israelites looked different from others vision. He showed his people what will be God's vision if they follow fully and informed them how God will punish if they do not follow. Not many leaders have such vision. Such vision helps followers to obey or disobey. (Deuteronomy 18:1, 15)

A vision is foundation for leadership success. David was a great visionary and his vision was beyond Saul ever imagined. David's vision brought great benefit for Israelites- vision united, vision provided a center for leadership, vision dominated

> **Vision without action is a daydream.**
>
> **Action without vision is a nightmare.**
>
> **Vision plus Action is Progress.**
>
> **Act today is sync with tomorrow's Vision**

inner conversation, vision inspired greatness and vision attracted others to the leaders.

"Catch the vision and run with it" – Rick Farley

Grant Bernard [3] says, *"don't hang around visionless leaders"* It is important to keep company with those who are successful. If you hang around people who do not have vision, eventually it will impair your vision also. Once this happens, the people whom you lead will slowly begin to perish.

"He who walks in integrity walks securely."

Chapter 10

Integrity

The integrity of the upright guides them,
but the unfaithful are destroyed by their duplicity.
(Proverbs 11:3)

Integrity – Demonstrating trustworthiness
by doing what is right and saying what is true

Integrity means honesty and more. It refers to having strong internal guiding principles that one does not compromise on. It also means treating others as you would wish to be treated. Integrity is the quality of being morally good. Integrity is a quality which includes-honesty, dependability, uprightness, loyalty and sincerity. Integrity springs from a persons ethical and spiritual convictions.

The character of integrity implies; honesty, sincerity, purity, virtue and fairness.

Leaders are regularly battered by circumstances, by Satan, and by their own people. All good leaders must demonstrate that they can take it without losing composure. People are drawn to strength of character, and tend to believe what strong people say. While they may feel sympathetic towards the weak, they tend not to follow them. This does not mean leaders should pretend they are not suffering, but that their determination and integrity dictate that they maintain consistency even in the face of suffering. It also means that a leader would continue to pursue the right goals and live for God, even if no one else follows.

It is believed that a solid sense of right, wrong, and strong guiding principles is the most essential and basic leadership character or skill. Integrity is skill to the extent that we see in action. A good leader is not afraid of rejection by his/her followers because his / her concern is doing what is right, not being followed. Jesus taught that the good shepherd "goes out before them" which means that such a shepherd sets a course knowing that the sheep will follow after. When people sense that a leader is more concerned, about being followed than about what God wants, they grow cynical about following. Most people are suspicious of leaders anyway, and will test leaders by threatening not to follow. Only when they see that a leader cannot be manipulated will they realize their choice is to follow or to take their chances elsewhere. Integrity is equally important in big and small things. Any break in moral principle can create crack in leadership integrity.

Integrity is most important ingredient in leadership. Leaders need to understand integrity well, develop and practice to be successful. Being a person of integrity means, to do what you know is true. Many times leaders try to change another person's behavior, while having the same problem themselves. A man of integrity watches his/her words carefully and makes sure that whatever s/he preaches, s/he practices. If s/he preaches humility and honesty, s/he should show that s/he practices it also . Integrity promotes trust and not much is accomplished without trust.

Integrity includes self-discipline of a leader. It implies personal conduct, focusing on worthy goals instead of distractions. Self-discipline in leader's life is investable because it inspires orderliness, punctuality, thriftiness and resourcefulness.

Noah was a righteous man. He loved God with his whole heart and was honest to God's call. From Noah's life, we can learn that it is possible to be faithful, honest and please God even in the midst of a corrupt and sinful generation. Surely, it was not easy to Noah but he obeyed sincerely and honestly.

Paul spoke of his failures and success with openness, only few leaders practice these days. Even before his conversion he served God sincerely, with great integrity (2 Timothy 1:3), and with great personal integrity. Integrity and sincerity are qualities of leadership, were part of God's law for the Israelites (Deuteronomy 18:13). God wants His people to show transparent character.

David wrote this prayer

"May integrity and uprightness protect me,
because my hope is in you?" *(Psalms 25:21).*

Solomon says

"He who walks in integrity walks securely."
Therefore, integrity is sincerity of heart and intention, truthfulness, uprightness, being sincere, honest and pure heart in all your intentions.

Joseph was also a man of integrity and high moral character. Joseph refused his master's wife's desire to go to bed with her, the consequence was painful and ultimately prison. A leader can learn more than one lesson here. Joseph was honest to his master, sincere in his duty and not tempted or attracted for physical pleasure.

Paul was a determined leader even who shared the gospel while he was in prison.Paul showed his high degree of integrity while he criticized his fellow believer Peter. He criticized Peter's hypocrisy and demanded that all Christian leaders remain consistent, regardless of the company they keep. From Paul we can learn lesson on criticism:[1]

- Check your motives before your criticism. The goal should be to help not humiliate
- Make sure the issue is worthy of criticism
- Be specific. Do not drop hints, but clearly name the problem
- Don't undermine the person's self-confidence or identity. Make it obvious that you value the person
- Do not postpone needed criticism. If the same is big, act now
- Look at yourself looking at others. Take the log out of your own eye
- End criticism with encouragement. Finish on a positive note.

Very few leaders have guts to invite their followers to evaluate their leadership like Job.

"Teach me, and I will be quiet;
show me where I have been wrong" (Job 6:24).

Only a leader with strong character and a strong sense of security, positive motive and conscience can do this. A leader must be strong enough to admit his/her mistakes, smart enough to learn from them, and strong enough to correct them.

How many Christian leaders have this kind of character — integrity?

"For people, who hate discipline and only get more stubborn,
there will come a day when life tumbles in and they break,
but by then it will be too late to help them" (Proverbs 29:1).

Many leaders ruined their lives and damaged others' lives because of lack of integrity. Character becomes crucial issue in leader's life. It is necessary to strike balance between character and ability, of course, both are necessary for development. John Maxwell has shown how to balance.[2]

What I am	What I do	What I can
Humble	*Rely on God*	*Power from God*
Visionary	*Set Goals*	*High Morale*
Convicted	*Do the Right Thing*	*Credibility*

It is better to look at the future than the past. Never build your future around your past. God never sees your past to decide your future. Stop looking at where you were or have been but start looking at where you are going. While leaders try to maintain integrity, they have to overcome questionable background. Jesus overcame the stigma of a questionable background-His birth.

"Brothers, I do not consider myself yet to have taken hold of it. But one thing I do: Forgetting what is behind and straining toward what is ahead, I press on toward the goal to win the prize for which God has called me heavenward in Christ Jesus". *(Philippines 3:13-14).*

Live in peace with one another.

Chapter 11

Team Builder

Your team members are your friends not servants.
"No longer do I call you servants, but I have called you friends"
(John 15:15)

"Live in peace with one another"
(1 Thessalonians 5:13)

Team building is an art of working together to create beneficial results. Team building also refers to the selection and motivation of team, that it involves undertaking various activities that improves the overall performance of the team. A team should have a motivating factor in order to perform and self-assess.

No one-person can do all, therefore, a team comprises of others with different skills is essential for an organization. In a team, connecting people is very critical, if you want to influence and grow your organization. A great leader always contacts and connects people to go with him/her, and then alone you can expect people to move to new heights with healthy relationship.

"He who thinks he leads and has not one
following him is only taking walk" (Anonymous)

Why team building?

1. To promote progress
2. To achieve better efficiency
3. Closer relations and cooperation among the team
4. To develop and encourage one another.
5. To develop interdependence or bring unity

The importance of Team Building;

1. For better communication
2. Easy to motivate workers
3. Promote creativity
4. Identify team's strengths and weaknesses
5. Improve the ability to solve problems
6. Break barriers
7. Develop better relations
8. Increase efficiency and effectiveness

Outstanding leaders appeal to the hearts of their followers, not their minds. A leader must know how to build and nurture such a team. A good leader knows when to be a leader and when to be a follower. The best leaders are good followers. Building teamwork is another essential leadership skill. The task of the leader is to get his/her people from where they are, to where they have not been. Henry Kissinger knew that it was no great feat to get others to do something they had done before. Real leadership skill is getting them to do something they have not ever done or are not sure is possible.

When you wish to play together as a team, you have to care for one another, believe and love each other. It is wonderful when the people believe in their leader; but it is more wonderful when the leader believes in the people. Strong leaders are effective at bringing others together in a team. This is often the difference between leaders and others, who also get good ideas, but never have much impact on the Body of Christ. Bringing people together and helping them overcome barriers, to understanding, personal resentments, jealousies, and prejudice is typical work for leaders. "Leadership is getting people to work for you when they are not obligated" (Fred Price) Good leaders often engage in conflict management with peaceful results. Those who try to manage conflict between others but end up fanning the flames or consistently repudiating one or the other party in conflict, usually cannot lead for long, or at least must have a small following.

Team building also means that the leader is a consensus leader. He is able to get more than one person to agree about key values or directions of movement. Team members always love and admire a person, who is able to help them to another level, someone who enlarges them and empowers them to be successful. If a leader demonstrates competency, genuine concern for others, and admirable character, people will follow (T. Richard Chase).

A good team builder always enlarges its value to the team, improves the team value and makes each team member valuable. One of the greatest gifts leaders can give to those around them is hope. Never underestimate its power. The sign of great leaders is not what they accomplish on their own, but what they accomplish through the team. Therefore, never work alone. No matter how much work you can do, no matter how engaging your personality may be, you will not advance far in business if you cannot work through others (John Craig).

A good team builder is one who has faith, confidence, friendly, encouraging, unselfish and generous with his /her team members. He/She should be supervisor not super worker.

Team members, always love and admire a person who is able to help them to another level, someone who enlarges them and empowers them to be successful. The success of a leader depends upon his/her influence and his /her productivity on the leaders he or she prepares. A leader has to identify and develop potential team members, this will not only help the team members but leaders will greatly benefit. "The best executive is the one who has sense enough to pick good men to do what he wants done, and self-restraint to keep from meddling with them while they do it" (Theodore Roosevelt). Spending time and resources on members' development should be considered as an investment. Remember you cannot push anyone up the leadership ladder unless s/he is willing to climb. A leader must be willing to go alone forward, before s/he asks others to follow.

John Maxwell says leadership begins in the heart. Therefore, understand, love, and help your people.Building relationship depends on love.

"I no longer call you servants,
because a servant does not know his master's business.
Instead, I have called you friends,
for everything that I learned from my Father I
have made known to you."
(John 15:15)

David had the quality of creating leaders. While he was at Ziklag, his men were diverse, loyal and hungry for victory, he trained them in his likeness – he was rational, he was resourceful, he was rewarding and he was respectable (John Maxwell).

David's men like Adino, Eleazar and Shammah caught the same vision David had for lives and for all Israel. They strengthened themselves together with David. These men followed David because he was a man of honor, integrity and caring. To be a successful and effective leader like David you recognize the necessity of having other like-minded people with you, who can share your vision and work towards a common goal. Other two great qualities one can learn from David are, putting the interest of others first and leading by example.

Nehemiah had the skill of organizing team building. The people were discouraged and tired and opposition was making life miserable. He harnessed the strength of the family unit, ordering half a family to work while the other half stood guard and rested. The people recovered their courage as Nehemiah solved real problems through decisive action – team building. He practiced a wise delegation of responsibility and he gave recognition to subordinate leaders (Nehemiah 2). Leaders should be aware of the principle 'right man at right place'.

Joshua could capture Jericho only by convincing and building a team with capacities required for the purpose.

"It is capacity to develop and improve their skills
that distinguishes leaders from their followers"
(Warren Bennis and Bert Nanus)

People followed Joshua because he had faith, confidence and a friendly and great character of team building.

All leaders need faithful friends however, the leader is great and powerful. Even David needed Jonathan for strength and encouragement to escape from Saul's dangerous plan to kill him. A good friend is always a blessing. Jonathan risked his life to help David and remained his friend until the end of life.

With good leaders everything improves because he transfers ownership of work to his team, encourages, improves their confidence and performance, makes them think, gives opportunity to improve their skills and creates a harmonious environment. When leaders exercise their authority without servant's heart, s/he will hurt himself, his/her team and organization. Therefore, exercise authority with wisdom and caution, lead others by serving, not bossing them and recognize no human control life except God. As Fred Smith says,

...my (leadership) responsibility is to be a supervisor, not a super worker.

A good team leader gives myself away and cultivates an attitude of selflessness. S/He begins by – being generous, avoiding internal politics, displaying loyalty and valuing interdependence more than himself.[1]

A leader has to choose inner circle with great care. A good leader is one who has the sense enough to pick good men and women to do what s/he wants, and self-restraint enough to keep from meddling with them while they do it. David's leadership success was because of his /her faithful inner circle, which s/he built even though some of them were misfit initially. David transformed and made winning team. Therefore, David was a great team builder and his team made him great king.

A leader should be aware of the swing in an organization, see that better players join the organization than are leaving. This demands that a leader has to take care of those closest to him/her. Every team has three groups of players – starters, bench players and core group. Leader's responsibility is to see each group continually develops. If your treatment of key people doesn't match their value, you run the risk of losing them.[2]

Jesus was comfortable in the presence of anglers, wise men, poor and rich, women or men or children. He was at ease with all of these. Jesus never discriminated. Jesus knew that every person has the required potential, Jesus broke tradition. Therefore, a leader has to treat people right and never pre-judge. Only fools make permanent decisions without knowledge.[3]

Spending time with the best of your team or inner circle is crucial for a leader.

After six days Jesus took Peter, James and John with him and
led them up a high mountain, where they were all alone.
There he was transfigured before them. (Mark 9:2).

Jesus took them on a special mission to reveal his connection with father God.

Every Christian leader can learn from these great leaders a lesson for team building even during difficult times.

There is nothing more unpleasant than, when morale is low. This means the team is negative, lethargic and without hope. When team's morale is low, then do the following:[4]

– *Investigate the situation*

– *Initiate belief*

– *Create energy*

– *Communicate hope*

> **No man will make a great leader who wants to do it all himself or to get all the credit for doing it** – Andrew Carnage.

"Lead good people down a wrong path and you will come
to a bad end; do good and you will be rewarded for it."
(Proverbs 28:10)

A good navigator will have vision for his/her destination, he or she understands what it will take to get there, and he or she knows whom he or she will need on the team to be successful. Good leaders can recognize the obstacles long before they appear on the scene.

> **"Live in peace with one another:** I Thessalonians 5:13

Successful leaders build teams without forgetting that every team member's role is contributing to the bigger achievement. Winston Churchill was successful with his passionate appeal to the coal miners during World War II.[5]

One of the important roles of the leader in a team is to mentor her/his team members. Jesus was a master teacher and mentor.

No one was born with great knowledge. You become what you are. You discover what you know. Every song needs a singer. Every achiever needs motivation. Every student needs a teacher – Mike Murdock. It is therefore, every successful team needs a great mentor. Take time to train, it always takes time. Your team will remember what you teach.

Leaders have to be selected well and build right ones as Jesus selected and prepared 12 disciples and Moses trained Joshua. How can we build leaders then?[6] Malcolm Webber suggests certain guidelines for new or emerging leaders:

- Look beyond appearance and be willing to take some risks
- Do not be in a hurry
- Pray much before the choice is made
- Consider the fruit of the existing leadership
- Examine the recommendation of those around
- Look for security in Christ
- Look for the willingness to serve and to make personal sacrifices for the Divine cause
- Look for a genuine love for God's people
- Look for responsibility
- Look for accountability
- Look for the ability to learn from experience
- Look for 'big-picture' thinking

- Look for "outside the box" thinking
- Look for a desire to help others succeed
- Look for a realistic opinion of him and others
- Ask yourself if you are the right one to help this emerging leader
- Make necessary adjustments
- Don't demand perfection

"He who leads the upright along an evil path will fall into his own trap, but the blameless will receive a good inheritance."

(Proverbs 28:10).

The servant leadership is servant first,...It begins with the natural feeling that one wants to serve to serve first.

Chapter 12

Servant-Leader

"Instead whoever wants to become great among
you must be your servant, and whoever wants to be
first must be your slave-just as the Son of Man did not
come to be served, but to serve, and to give his life
as a ransom for many
(Matthew 20:26-28)

"When he had finished washing their feet, he put on
his clothes and returned to his place."Do you understand?
what I have done for you?" he asked them, "You call me
'Teacher' and 'Lord,' and rightly so, for that is what I am.
Now that I, your Lord and Teacher, have washed your feet,
you also should wash one another's feet. I have set you an
example that you should do as I have done for you
(John 13:12-15)

Who is a servant leader? A servant leader is someone who is servant first, who has responsibility to be in the world, and so he or she contributes to the well-being of people and community. A servant looks to the needs of the people, and asks him/her how he or she can help them to solve problems and promote personal development. Servant leader places his/her main focus on people, because only content and motivated people are able to reach their targets and to fulfill the set expectations. Servant leader is one who first wants to serve and not be served. In spiritual leadership, God's touch in leadership should be seen. Without God's touch leaders words, actions or even motivational seminars, looks like classroom teaching.

Jesus himself best defined servant leadership.

> *"Whoever wants to become great among you must be your servant,*
> *and whoever wants to be first must be your slave – just as the*
> *Son of Man did not come to be served, but to serve,*
> *and to give his life as a ransom for many"*
> (Matthew 20:26-28).

Jesus modeled the true servant style of leadership. He, the lord incarnate, bent down and washed their feet, teaching them the true measures of leading by first serving others (John 13:12-17). The term servant speaks of low power, low prestige, low respect and low honor. Most people are not attracted for low-value and low profile jobs.

Servant leadership is both a leadership philosophy and set of leadership practices. Servant leadership includes both individuals and organizations, which have faith and bring a change. There are many who want to exercise authority but few who want to take the towel and basin and wash another's feet. Paul reminds us that our attitude is to be like Christ's, in that we consider others better than they consider ourselves and nothing out of selfishness; rather we look out for the interests of others. From a biblical perspective, servant leadership is not only being free of abuse of power but is primarily based on mutual respect and love for one another. In Christianity, all leadership should be servant leadership.

In the words of Robert K. Grenleaf servant leadership can be defined:

> "The servant leadership is servant first...It begins with the natural feeling that one wants to serve to serve first. Then conscious choice brings one to aspire to lead. That person is sharply different from one who is leader first, perhaps because of the need to assuage an unusual power drive or to acquire material possessions... The leader-first and the servant first are two extreme types. Between them there are shadings and blends that are part of the infinite variety of human nature". "The difference manifests itself in the care taken by the servant-first to make sure that other people's highest priority needs are being served. The best test, and difficult to administer is: Do those served grow as persons? Do they, while being served, become healthier, wiser, freer, more autonomous, more likely themselves to become servants? And, what is the effect on the least privileged in society? Will they benefit or at least not be further deprived?"

John Mott, captured well the heart of spiritual leadership as follows.

> "Leadership in the sense of rendering service, leadership in the sense of the largest unselfishness, in the sense of full hearted absorption in the greatest work of the world, building up the kingdom of our Lord Jesus Christ"

The concept servant leadership is mentioned in ancient and religious texts. In Christianity, the passage from the Gospel of Mark is often mentioned of servant leadership.

"But Jesus called them (his disciples) to himself and said to them,

> "You know that those who are considered rulers over the Gentiles lord it over them and their great ones exercise authority over them. Yet it shall not be so among you; but whoever desires to become great among you shall be your servant. And whoever of you desires to be first shall be slave of all. For even the son of Man did not come to be served, but to serve, and to give His life a ransom for many" (Mark 10:42-45).

Islam believes *"the leader of a people is their servant"*

Chanakya wrote in his book 'Arthashastra',..

> The king (leader) shall consider as good, not what pleases himself but what pleases his subjects (followers) the king (leader) is a paid servant and enjoys the resources of the state together with people"

The Chinese sage Lao Tzu wrote The Tao Te Ching, a simple treatise on servant leadership as:

> *The great leader forgets her/him and attends to the development of others.*
> *Good leaders support the bottom ten percent.*
> *Great leader know that the diamond in the rough"*
> *Is always found "in the rough*

In most cultures, it is emphasized in the history, holistic, co-operative, communal, intuitive, caring and spiritual values in servant leadership.

The leadership in the context of servant leadership can be three styles of leadership – autocratic, participative and Laissez-faire.

Servant leadership can be associated with participative leadership style. The authoritarian style will not be in harmony with servant leadership style. The priority of servant leadership is to encourage, support and enable subordinates to unfold their full potential and abilities. It is therefore, in servant leadership there is more scope for delegation of responsibilities and participative decision-making. If you wish to be a leader, you will be frustrated, for very few people wish to be led. If you aim to be a servant, you will never be frustrated.

Servant leaders desire to invest in others to see the vision accomplished. Jesus' hope was for his followers to do "great things" than he had accomplished (John 14:12). Moreover, the period of his vision was future; it was only after his ascension that his followers "turned the world upside down" (Acts 17:6). Thus, he was not merely doing things for his own accomplishment now. He built others for their accomplishments to the future. (Malcolm Webber, p. 24)

Servant hood is not about position or skill of a leader, but it is about attitude. The truth is, best leaders serve others before they serve themselves. According to John Maxwell true servant leader are those who:

- Put others ahead of their own agenda
- Possess the confidence to serve
- Initiate service to others
- Are not position-conscious
- Serve out of love.

Leaders need to know that their influence has less to do with position or title, than it does with life's attitude. More than position the leadership result and credibility are vital. Leaders gain credibility when their actions speak and when they add value to others.

A servant leader has to have high degree of credibility. King David was no doubt a great leader but he lost his credibility, when he turned to a married woman and killed her husband. David was in the habit of picking and choosing when he would listen to God. King Solomon also lost his leadership credibility, when he did not listen to God and the counsel of his advisors and took many wives and allowed them to worship other gods.

Most scholars agree that servant leader need to have following characteristics to serve as servant. Robert K. Grenleaf is recognized as a father of servant leadership mentions following characteristics of servant.

1. Listening
2. Empathy
3. Healing
4. Awareness
5. Persuasion
6. Conceptualization
7. Foresight
8. Stewardship

9. Commitment to the growth of people

10. Building community

Try to forget yourself in the service of others. For when we think too much of our own interests, and ourselves we really become despondent. But when we work for others, our efforts return to bless us. (Sidney Powell)

In servant leader, one should:

> A great man is always willing to be little
>
> Ralph Waldo Emerson

1. Have a sense of call

2. Put others ahead of their own agenda

3. Possess confidence to serve

4. Initiate service to others

5. Not position conscious

6. Serve out of love

Joshua's preparedness for the responsibilities of leadership, are evidenced by the fact that because of his unswerving loyalty and devotion, he is called the servant of Moses. Joshua was loyal to God and Moses, because he faithfully obeyed the authority and maintained committed relationship.

A leader, who is loyal to his authority, will be inspired by virtues like obedience, dependability, supportiveness and commitment.

Servant leader will have a character of humility, honoring others by drawing attention to them instead of self. Humility inspires honor, attentiveness, flexibility, meekness. Humility also means is to make a right estimate of one's self.

Attitude can turn our problems into blessings.

Chapter 13

Good and Right Attitude

We have different gifts, according to the grace given us.
If a man's gift is ...leadership, let him govern diligently
(Romans 12:6)

In matters of style, swim with the current.
In matters of principle, stands like a rock.
T. Jefferson

Attitude is a complex mental state involving beliefs and feelings and values and dispositions to act in certain ways.

- Right attitude comes first
- Attitude determines our approach of life
- Attitude is often the only difference between success and failure
- Attitude at the beginning of a task will affect its outcome more than anything else
- Attitude can turn our problems into blessings

King David one of the Bible's greatest leader, was able to motivate men and pour his attitude and skills into his team. His team exercised proper leadership attitude and actions that helped David become Israel's greatest warrior and leader.

As a king of Judah son of David did what was right in the eyes of Lord. He expelled the male shrine prostitutes from land and got rid of all the idols his fathers had made. His action not only exemplifies his obedience to the Lord but looked things with right attitude. (1 Kings 15: 11-12)

Right attitude and right time are important for right decisions for a leader. Ordinary people, only think how they shall spend their time, while a man of talent thinks of how to use it. Killing time is not murder but suicide.

For a leader, time is everything. Nehemiah had the right attitude and took right decisions and right time to approach the King to build the wall of Jerusalem. He took almost three months in prayer and preparing plan. If a leader has the right attitude, right time for right decision, he will have better chance of success (Nehemiah 2).

Then Caleb quieted the people before Moses, and said,

> "Let us go up at once and take possession, for we are well able to overcome it. But the men who had gone up with him said, "We are not able to go up against the people for they are stronger than we". (Numbers 13:30-31).

This incident tells us the difference of attitude. In leadership, attitudes makes a big difference, therefore, to be an effective leader, positive attitude is essential. Caleb and Joshua exhibited their positive and optimist attitude and at the end, they were successful. The lessons a leader can learn from Caleb and Joshua can be:[1]

– Our attitude determines our approach of life

– Our attitude determines our relationship with people

- Our attitude is often the only difference between success and failure

- Our attitude at the beginning of a task will affect its outcome more than anything else

- Our attitude can turn problems into blessings

- Our attitude is not automatically good just because we belong to God.

Leaders with right attitude should be ready to learn all the time.

Everyone who competes in the games goes into strict training
(1 Corinthians 9:25)

Every leader wishes to achieve his/her goals as fast as possible, but forget to be fit to achieve. People, who are fit and clear in their goals, will do whatever the circumstances. Leaders who wish to improve always follow preparation, contemplation (self-improvement) and application.[2] (John Maxwell p.213).

Your attitude is a little thing, but it makes a big difference. Look backwards with gratitude, upward with confidence and forward with hope.

No leader is above vision of an organization and God's purpose. If a leader thinks out of his/her pride and forgets his/her commitment, His/her pride will swallow as per John Maxwell. Good leader needs to respect God's purpose, organization's vision and leadership.

> **Your attitude is a little thing, but it makes a big difference.**
>
> **Look backwards with gratitude, upward with confidence and forward with hope.**
>
> **It all depends on how you look at things and not how they are.**
>
> **A new attitude might improve your career prospect.**

An attitude of prayer is essential in a leader's life. A leader also needs team members who have deep relationship with God, possesses faith and loyal servant of God. Leader has to say, "We can do this. With God we can handle it". Only man of prayer, a wo/man who has a deep and abiding relationship with God will be able to produce and maintain this kind of attitude of prayer.

Leader's attitude of diligence is important requirement. Diligence can be described as willingly completing the task that is accepted.

The question of leadership is the concept of power and the leader's attitude to it. Leaders are the trustee of power for the time being because power belongs to the people. Power without moral yardstick might lead to misuse. There is an Urdu couplet, which says, "Intoxication of liquor leaves you, but intoxication of power continues to grow, takes hold of you and finally drowns you" (R. M. Lala).

Lala, believes leader's attitude of power will determine his attitude to people. If his passion is power, he will use people as pawns. If his passion is people, he will do the best for them. He will use his power to give them the benefits that are their due. He will govern with compassion and concern.

Great things are done more through
courage than through wisdom.

Chapter 14

Courage, Confidence and Decisiveness

The greatest test of courage on earth is to bear defeat without losing heart.
Often the test of courage is not to die but to live.
A man of courage is also full of faith.
Life shrinks or expands in proportion to your courage.
Great things are done more through courage than through wisdom
(Anonymous)

Courage is a quality of mind, which enables one to encounter dangerous difficulties with firmness or without fear or failing of heart, valor, and boldness. Confidence means freedom from doubt, belief in you. Courage is also defined as bravery. The opposite of courage is to submit to fear. Courage is essential ingredient to establish leadership. There are different kinds of courage – moral, spiritual, spontaneous and unprepared courage.

Courage is a prime requisite of leadership. Lord Moran, personal physician to Sir Winston Churchill found soldiers who could be placed broadly in one of four categories:[1]

- *Men who did not feel fear*
- *Men who felt fear but did not show it*
- *Men who felt fear, showed it, but did their job*
- *Men who felt fear, showed it and shirked*

"Be strong and of good courage" (Deuteronomy 31:7).

Leaders, who act boldly during crises and changes, will find followers. Courage is willingness to overcome fear and plan to move ahead. Courage, confidence and decisiveness are most important qualities of a Christian leader. Lack of courage, demonstrates weakness and delay in decision making, which might invite problems. Courage means ability to control fear when facing danger or pain. Courage can be defined as the ability and commitment to endure and challenge difficulty or danger with firmness in spite of fear. Courage is significant for the development and success of an organization. Courageous decision should be wise, because it involves challenge. John Maxwell[2] suggests following truths about courage:

- *Courage begins with an inward battle*
- *Courage is making thing right, not just smoothing them over*
- *Courage in a leader inspires commitment from followers.*
- *Courage by a leader inspires*
- *Your life expands in proportion to your courage*

Whenever we see progress in an organization, it is because the leaders took courageous decisions. Courage gives leadership position. A leader in an organization is not always the smartest or most creative person on the team. He or she is not also necessarily the first to identify an opportunity. A leader is the one who has the courage to initiate to set things in motion and move ahead.

David can be the best example when he showed his courage, capability, strong confidence and right decision to fight with Goliath. God gave him victory and David in turn gave Him all the credit and glory. David exhibited his bravery and gave an entire army something which was lacking, courage. David was courageous and careful in taking risk. No leader can be successful without taking a risk. Leaders cannot take risks without courage, therefore, courage essential for leadership.

Courage and confidence should come from God. David said to Philistine (Goliath)

"You come against me with sword and spear and javelin, but I come against you in the name of the LORD Almighty, the God of the armies of Israel, whom you have defied. This day the LORD will hand you over to me, and I'll strike you down and cut off your head. Today I will give the carcasses of the Philistine army to the birds of the air and the beasts of the earth, and the whole world will know that there is a God in Israel.

(1 Samuel 17: 45-46)

David triumphed because of his courage, confidence in God and took a right decision and a right time. Help is largely given to the people of courage. One of the greatest pleasures of life is doing the things that others say you cannot do. I am sure David experience greatest pleasure after he killed Goliath.

God said to Moses…

Be strong and courageous. Do not be afraid or terrified because of them, for the Lord your God goes with you, he will never leave you nor forsake you."

Then Moses summoned Joshua and said to him in the presence of all Israel,

Be strong and courageous, for you must go with this people into the land that the Lord swore to their forefathers to give them, and you must divide it among them as their inheritance. The Lord himself goes before you and will be with you; he will never leave you nor forsake you. Do not be afraid, do not be discouraged

Here we see that Moses and Joshua both had courage and confidence to follow God's order. (Deuteronomy 31:6-8)

Nehemiah develops courage and confidence and made clear decisions to build the wall of Jerusalem (Nehemiah 3). People ridiculed him but he was determined to build the wall. One of the greatest pleasures of life is doing the things that others say you cannot do.

Abraham and Sarah left Ur full of hope and confidence that God will guide them.

> **Dream (courageous) what you dare to dream.**
> *Go where you want to go.*
> *Be what you want to be.*
> *Believe in yourself and others will too*

Esther was willing to break Persian protocol and walk into the king's presence with confidence and hope.

These people were able to accomplish what they wished, because of courage, hope and confidence.

Paul says to Corinthians,

"Be on your guard, stand firm in the faith, be men of courage, be strong.
Do everything in love"
(1 Corinthians 16:13-14).

A man of courage is also full of faith like Paul.

The following night the Lord stood near Paul and said,

"Take courage! As you have testified me in
Jerusalem, so you must also testify in Rome"
(Acts 23:11)

Often the test of courage is not to die but to live. A Christian leader needs to do what is right in the sight of God, despite what his/her followers say or believe. Faith, hope, charity, all the rest do not become virtue until it takes courage to exercise them.

God said to Jacob, So do not fear, for I am with you; do not be dismayed, for I am your God. I will strengthen you and help you; I will uphold you with my righteous right hand. (Isaiah 41:10)

Andy Stanley[3] suggests three expressions of courage that often elude leaders:

1. The courage to say no
2. Courage to face current reality
3. Courage to dream

Dependable leader means a reliable leader. Persistent leader is one who continues doing something in spite of difficulty or opposition.

Let us not become weary in doing good, for at the proper time we will reap a harvest if we do not give up. (Galatians 6:9)

In a successful leaders life dependability and persistence are equally important, as of courage and confidence. Perseverance is the act or state of persisting in anything undertaken, continued pursuit. Success does not come to the weak and those who give up, when it is hard to achieve. Success comes to those who are persistent, aggressive and want to grow.

A Christian leader must be dependable and who is capable of handling his/her own affairs as well as the affairs of others. There is no dependence that can be sure but, a dependence upon one's self. The followers always look, whether their leaders are dependable, they will share their problems, listen to him/her and trust him/her.

Followers also expect that leaders should lead them in chaotic and uncertain situation

Joseph labored as slave with great humility and won the confidence of his master because he was dependable.

Jacob wrestled with the angel all night, and did not give up until he received the blessing he was looking for. Moses, Joshua, Nehemiah and David all had character of dependability, perseverance, aggressive and desire to excel.

Persistence prevails when all else fail. Persistence and achievement go hand in hand. Persistence is the ultimate gauge of leadership. Nehemiah is great example. Nehemiah faced opposition and resistance, yet he took challenges with great patience and persistence character by relying on God, respecting the opposition, encouraging weak and his faithful people. One of greatest character of a leader is how one handles the opposition; Nehemiah handled opposition with great skill.

Jesus said,

"No man, having put his hand to the plough and looking back, is fit for the kingdom of God" (Luke 9:62)

"Never mistake knowledge for wisdom. One helps you make a living; the other helps you make a life."

Chapter 15

Intelligent and Wise

Let the wise listen and add to their learning,

And let the discerning get guidance

(Proverbs 1:5)

Intelligent is one who has the capacity for thought and reason, especially to a high degree and possessing sound knowledge or showing sound good judgment. Wise leaders will have or are prompted by wisdom. *"Never mistake knowledge for wisdom. One helps you make a living; the other helps you make a life." Lester R. Bittel*

Intelligent leaders should have the ability to gain and apply knowledge and skills. Intelligent leaders are also good at learning and understanding. A wise leader shows his/her experience, knowledge and good judgment. *As a rule he/she who has most information will have greatest success in life - Disraeli*

Leaders are proud of their intelligence and talent. They believe their talent is enough to gain success. What is more important is not intelligence but leader's attitude.

You have brilliant ideas, but if you can't get them across,
your ideas won't get you anywhere. – Lee Iacocca.

Successful leaders always initiate with a step to gain hearts of people before asking for a hand wisely. The ability of a leader depends upon his/her sincere commitment, experience and wisdom.

People expect wise words of advice, guidance from their leaders. Leader who uses his/her words skillfully can increase influence and achieve success. John Maxwell[1] believes that wise leaders work for justice, speaks of hope for the future, speaks with wisdom and save others from ruin, knows silence is powerful than words depending on the situation. Leader's words should feed and nourish their followers.

Christian leaders need to remember that …

'The fear of the Lord is the beginning of wisdom" (Psalm 111:10).
"God alone is wise" (Romans 16:27).

After becoming king, Solomon sought from God, to distinguish between right and wrong. The Lord appeared to Solomon in a dream by night; and God said,

"Ask for whatever you want me to give you." Solomon answered,
"You have shown great kindness to your servant, my father David,
because he was faithful to you and righteous and upright in heart.
You have continued this great kindness to him and have given him a son
to sit on his throne this very day.
So give your servant a discerning heart to govern your people and to
distinguish between right and wrong.
For who is able to govern this great people of yours?

1 King 2:5-6 and 9

Achieving good judgment skills and ethical sensitivity is the most important requirement of a leader, if one wishes to become an effective leader. (1 Kings 3:9). Christian leaders need wisdom, fear, and faith in God. Prayer opens us to God's wisdom and guidance. Respect and obedience to the Lord is first in leadership life.

Wise leaders share their lives with the people they serve. Wise leaders are not alone. Moses listened, to his father-in-law Jethro's advice by empowering others and delegating responsibility to trusted leaders with the community. He that walks with the wise men shall be wise. Wise leaders live in the community, they wish to build.

David wisely ignored when confronted and cursed by Shimel. An aide, Abishai, wanted to kill Shimel but David said, "Leave him alone, let him curse". Wisely ignoring a wrong is frequently desirable when one is a leader. (2 Samuel 16:11)

The prophet Ezekiel spoke against the king Tyre,

> By your wisdom and understanding, you have gained wealth for yourself and amassed gold and silver in your treasuries. By your great skill in trading you have increased your wealth, and because of your wealth your heart has grown proud. "'Therefore this is what the Sovereign LORD says: "'because you think you are wise, as wise as a god, I am going to bring foreigners against you, the most ruthless of nations; they will draw their swords against your beauty and wisdom and pierce your shining splendor. *(Ezekiel 28:4-7).*

Contrast this to the advice given to Israel's children.

Do not be wise in your own eyes; fear the LORD and shun evil
(Proverbs 3:7)

Wisdom alone is not enough; a leader has to have fear and faith in God.

A wise leader has to be always careful from where s/he gets his/her advice. John Maxwell has differentiated between wise and foolish leader. A foolish leader can be led astray by a corrupt inner circle:

- *The leader begins to browse for the wrong counsel*
- *The leader begins to listen to the wrong voices*
- *The leader joins the wrong inner circle*

A wise leader meditates on God's word day and night and results of receiving counsel from the right inner circle are:

- Stability
- Inward nourishment and refreshment
- Fruitfulness and productivity
- Strength and durability
- Success

He that walks with the wise men shall be wise.

Men don't follow titles; they follow courage.

Chapter 16

A Fighter

"Men don't follow titles; they follow courage!"
Mel Gibson.

L eaders often have to fight negative trends or false beliefs that develop within groups. Good leaders carefully consider before God, what factors are leading to the negative trends or views among their friends, and devise counter-measures. Leaders know that Satan launches attacks on the health of any group of fruitful Christians, and this knowledge leads to important conclusions.[1]

1. Individuals within the group are not the ultimate source of wrong thought and action because "we wrestle not with flesh and blood." Therefore, even propagators of wrong can be, and often are salvaged and rescued from their own foolishness. Look for good leaders to be co-workers with some who were in sin in the past and some who opposed them earlier. Of course, even the best leader will lose some who fall into error, and good leaders are willing to sustain such losses rather than go soft on God's standards.

2. Anticipating spiritual attack leads to watchfulness and alertness. Leaders are not always the first to discern a problem, but they are attentive to problems whether discovered by themselves or others.

> *"No situation is so bad but what some good can come from it"* **(Romans 8:28)**

3. Leaders know they have to fight in prayer and they bring others into this work.

Joshua followed God's instructions for the battle of Jericho. Because Joshua was obedient, God performed a miracle at the battle of Gibeon. God made the sun stand still in the sky for an entire day so the Israelites conquered the land of Canaan. Under Joshua's godly leadership, the Israelites conquered the land of Canaan. Joshua proved as a great fighter in prayer and faith, every leader has to learn this lesson.

David was courageous as a champion and great fighter. David, the brave shepherd boy fought the roaring lion and the wild bear. He made sure no harm came to his flock. When he met Goliath, the giant, he knew that only God could rescue him. His fight with Goliath the giant made him a marked man. God gave the victory and David gave Him all the glory.

The story of David and Goliath is a factual account from biblical history that demonstrates how the Lord intercedes for His people. David was filled with faith and a passion for God's name which was being blasphemed by Goliath; slew Goliath with a stone and a sling. David's faith was so strong that he was willing to believe that the Lord would go with him and enable him to defeat Goliath. David's faith was born out of his experience of God's grace and mercy in his life up to that point.

From David's story, we can learn that the God we serve is capable of defeating any of the giants in our lives – fear, depression, financial issues, and doubts of faith – if we know Him and His nature well enough to step out in faith. When we do not know what the future holds, we have to trust Him. Knowing God through His word will build our faith in Him. James, tells us to consider it pure joy when we encounter trials because they test our faith and develop patience and perseverance. When we are tested by these trials, we can stand up against any giant that comes to defeat us.[2]

Consider it pure joy, my brothers, whenever you face trials
of many kinds, because you know that the testing of
your faith develops perseverance. Perseverance must finish its work
so that you may be mature and complete, not lacking anything.

James 1:2-4

Do to others, as you would like them to do to you.

Chapter 17

A Helper

"No servant can serve two masters. Either he will hate the one and love the other, or he will be devoted to the one and despise the other. You cannot serve both God and Money."

"Do to others as you would like them to do to you" Luke 16:13

"Ask what I may do for you, before I am taken away from you?" Elisha said,

A helper is a person who contributes to the fulfillment of a need or furtherance of an effort or purpose. And a giver is someone who devotes himself/herself completely; there are no greater givers than those who give themselves.

Jesus taught that the heart of spiritual leadership is servant hood. People are attracted to those who have served them and helped them in the past, and will often follow their advice. Leaders will not feel they have to meet all needs in the church, but will regularly strip themselves to wash the saints' feet. People are suspicious of leaders who put on air and seem to feel they are too important to do commonplace of work. Such leaders forfeit influence.

> **You can never really help people by doing for them the things they can and should do themselves**

Nehemiah was empathetic; he listened to grievances of people and took remedial decisions. He let people cry on his shoulders. He sympathized with others. He had genuine concern for the welfare of others, was so obvious that even his enemies noticed it. He expressed his concern in fasting prayer and tears. Nehemiah identified with his people in their sorrow and in their sins.

King David recognized the needy and showed full compassion and extended kindness, restored their rights. He called Mephibosheth son of Jonathan and grandson of King Saul, he gave away all land that belonged to King Saul to Mephibosheth and invited Mephibosheth to eat at his table always. So Mephibosheth ate at David's table like one of the king's sons. What a generosity, compassion and help King David showed to someone whose grandfather wanted to kill him. (2 Samuel 9: 1-11).

A leader can be a mentor and needs mentoring, specially emerging leaders. Choose your mentor carefully. Elisha chooses Elijah as mentor. Therefore, it was, when they had crossed over, that Elijah said Elisha,

> When they had crossed, Elijah said to Elisha, "Tell me, what I can do for you before I am taken from you?" "Let me inherit a double portion of your spirit," Elisha replied. "You have asked a difficult thing," Elijah said, "yet if you see me when I am taken from you, it will be yours--otherwise not." (2 Kings 2:9-10)

Elisha and Elijah can be great examples and inspiration for every leader.

Encouragement is the oxygen of the soul.

Chapter 18

An Encourager

*"The task of leadership is not to put greatness
into people (team members), but to elicit it,
for the greatness is there already"*
(John Buchan)

An encourager is one who encourages, invites or stimulates to action, one who supplies incitement, either by counselor/ and reward.

"Encouragement is the oxygen of the soul"
(John Maxwell)

While it is possible to lead without encouraging, good leaders have learned to use this important spiritual tool. The Bible commands us to encourage one another, and a leader should show the way in this area. Leaders are those who, through encouragement, can restore confidence and enthusiasm to a group of people who are discouraged and depressed. Nothing great has been achieved without enthusiasm. Good leaders are constantly reminding people of their value, of God's love, of the promises of Scripture, and that failure is not the end of the world. Since followers are bound to fail often, the role of encourager, while not owned exclusively by leaders, is crucial to leaders' ability to maintain morale. Encouragement coming from a leader often has more impact for good than that coming from others. The world belongs to the enthusiast who keeps cool. A real leader, through actions and words, has the ability to encourage and motivate others to their highest level of achievement; then gives them the opportunity and freedom to grow.

"The task of leadership is not to put greatness into people (team members), but to elicit it, for the greatness is there already"
(John Buchan)

Nehemiah raised the morale of his colleagues, an important part of any leader's work. Nehemiah also encouraged others generously. He saw people were discouraged and demoralized. First, he kindled hope by testifying to the vision and providence of God, and then he secured their cooperation. (Nehemiah 2)

Deborah, a prophet, the wife of Lappidoth was leading Israel at the time Sisera a commander with great military strength had cruelly oppressed the Israelites for twenty years. She encouraged Barak to fight and she joined and with him, when Barak refused to go alone. Deborah, was courageous, and a leader of encouragement. (Judges 4:4-9)

Leaders also exhibit that s/he wants his/her team to grow and succeed not only by helping but make them believe that you genuinely wish them to be successful. Once people know this, they will believe you, follow you, help you and their commitment will enhance. Moses, Joshua, Nehemiah and David had this quality and were successful in making their people to believe.

David attracted men like him – souls in distress, ultimately became like him. David produced men like him – warriors and conquerors and attracted people who were weak in distress. Leaders need to remember, what you are what you produce. From David's leadership we can learn.[1]

   – *David attracted men even without pursuing them*

   – *David drew deep loyalty from them without over trying to get it*

   – *David transformed these men without disenchanting them over their initial state*

   – *David fought alongside these men and turned them into winners*

   All those who were in distress or in debt or discontented gathered around him, and he became their leader. About four hundred men were with him.

(1 Samuel 22:2)

Some leaders begin working with others on weakness rather than strength, because it is easy to see other people's problems and shortcoming. By doing so, you will demoralize and kill the energies in the process. However, if you put your energies on a positive aspect of a person you are dealing, you will bring out great talents and qualities of the person you are dealing for the organization. Leader has to work on weakness and encourage the qualities in his or her team.

Saul said to David,

   "You are not able to go out against this Philistine and fight him; you are only a boy, and he has been a fighting man from his youth."

(1 Sameul 17:33)

In situations like this, leader has to be wise and encourage his/her team member to utilize his /her talents and energies. Well, Saul here allowed David to fight with Goliath, out of helplessness or halfheartedly, not with much of encouragement.

Jesus offered incentives. Reward those who help you succeed. People are motivated by two forces, pain or pleasure; fear or reward, loss or gain. A leader can discipline with the rod or through reward system.

> *"And, behold, I come quickly, and my reward is*
> *with me, to give every man according as his*
> *work shall be" – Revelation 22:12.*

Lead and inspire people. Don't try to manage and manipulate people.
Inventories can be managed but people must be lead.

Ross Perot

Ironically, good leaders are also compromisers. While doggedness and determination are important, perfectionism works against effective leadership. We live in a fallen world where our visions will never be completely fulfilled. People never quite do what they should, and lives always present with the unexpected. As a result, leaders realize they need to get the best they can, while not insisting on perfection or even on complete agreement. Wise leaders realize that the closer they come to their goal, the better, and that any movement is better than no movement. They also realize that a following either must be very small, or must include those who have a slightly different view, even though in general agreement on the most important issues. Leaders also realize they must prioritize goals and they feel good when major goals are attained even though lesser goals are not. Leaders who fail to prioritize, or who are perfectionist, run the danger of eventually breaking themselves and those around them. They are poor at team building, and cannot negotiate

Today adaptability and flexibility are essential skills of a leader. A leader must move easily from one set of circumstances to the next and take them

> It is weak man who urges compromise, never the strong man.

all in stride, even when the circumstances are unexpected. A good leader has to embrace change and see it as opportunity. Adaptability and change is an important character and known as a critical skill.

Lord, when I am wrong make me willing to change; when I am right, makes me easy to live with. So strengthen me that the power of my example will far exceeds the authority of my rank.

(Pauline H. Peters)

Positive compromise from a leader can be accepted. Godly leaders like Joseph did not compromise with his master's wife. Mordecai, Daniel, could not compromise and refused to worship God's their kings recommended.

David was furious when Nabal refused help. David then decided to fight and kill Nabal. David wisely compromised with Nabal's wife Abilgail, accepted her gifts and avoided fight with Nabal (1 Samuel 25)

Before a compromise a leader should listen to God's advice, evaluate his/her options, find out what other members of team feel and finally ask your inner voice, whether to go for compromise or not.

A good leader takes a little more than their share of the blame and a little less than share of the credit.

Chapter 19

A Victorious Sufferer

Even though I walk through the valley of the shadow of death, I will fear
no evil, for you are with me; your rod and your staff, they comfort me

Psalms 23:4

A sufferer is one who suffers for the sake of principles. Those who lead suffer just like others, and often more than others do. The difference is that leaders can suffer with grace and even with thanksgiving. They remain focused and functional during times of suffering and do not lose confidence in their principles as much as others might. Leaders know how to avoid focusing only on their own suffering even during times of intense pain. They can keep their eye on the ball spiritually most of the time. People admire the heroism of those who can suffer without losing their trust in God or their commitment to others. They will ponder how to gain that ability for themselves and become willing to follow the leader as a result. Leaders who lose their composure too often or too completely when suffering usually forfeit influence with those they lead.

"A good leader takes a little more than their share of the blame
and a little less than share of the credit".

Moses' life is the finest example in the Bible. He could have lived as son/prince of Pharaoh and enjoyed privilege and pleasure of the palace. After murdering an Egyptian, he faced exile in the desert for forty years with sacrifice, until the God wanted him to become leader. Remember, every leader has to pay a price.

Moses was a very humble man, humbler than anyone else was. Moses suffered when Aaron and Miriam opposed. In spite of the opposition, Moses showed great love and generosity and asked God, to heal Miriam from leprosy.

Jesus, a great master leader had a quality of victorious sufferer. He was humiliated, suffered and crucified as per God's plan without any complaint or remorse. He was victorious sufferer because he was resurrected on the third day.

David too suffered in the hands of King Saul. Saul was jealous and afraid of David and therefore, he attempted to kill many times. Every time God saved David because He was with him. David finally became a king as a victorious sufferer.

Joseph had a tough life. His jealous brothers sold him into slavery. His boss's wife framed him because he refused to sleep with her and was thrown into prison. Because of his sincerity and trust in God, he became the leader of Egypt, second to Pharaoh. When there was famine, he saved his family and people of Egypt from starvation. God planed the events to put Joseph in a position to save them. Leaders should have vision to sustain through difficult circumstances.

How many Christian leaders have these qualities of suffering for others or organization?

When leader feel isolated, remember the truth of God and Psalms :

"Yea, though I walk through the valley of the shadow of death, I will fear no evil, for though art with me; thy rod and thy staff they comfort me" (Psalms 23:4).

The key to successful leadership today is influence, not authority.

Chapter 20

Influencer with Value

The key to successful leadership today is influence, not authority
Kenneth Blanchard

Influence is a power to affect persons or events. Ability to influence others to move in a particular direction is an important skill in leadership. Leadership also defined as the ability to persuade others to do something they might not have done without the leader's persuasion.

> "There have been meetings of only a moment which have left impressions for life... for eternity. No one can understand that mysterious thing we call 'influence' ... yet everyone of us continually exerts influence, either to heal, to bless, to leave marks of beauty; or to wound, to hurt. To poison, to stain other lives" (J.B. Miller)

Leadership is a relationship of trust where commitments flow from character and value. Leadership is a relationship of dependency upon people. Influence or persuasion is a good example of an essential leadership skill. Leadership ability is directly related to how much people trust you and how good your communication and relationships are. Someone is a leader when he/she influences other people, whether for good or bad. We lead others either whenever we cause others to change their behavior or attitudes, because they see our example and admire it, or because we persuade them with words to change. We can persuade more effectively after we carefully reflect before God, on what others need to change in their lives. Practice in persuasion and learning to show others, what they have to gain through change, are basic skills in leadership. In addition, personal investment into others' lives, leads to increased influence in those lives. Some leaders focus primarily on influencing those with whom they are deeply involved relationally, and depend on them to influence others.

Mordecai persuades and influenced Esther to go to the king and beg for mercy and plead with him to save her people, Israelites. This act of Mordecai, one can see as influence with great value.

Apollos was learned man, with thorough knowledge of scripture. He had been instructed in the way the Lord and he spoke with great fervor and taught/influenced about Jesus accurately. (Acts: 18:24-25).

Nehemiah was prayerful and an honest servant of King Artaxerxes. Being a servant, he influenced the king to help him build the wall of Jerusalem, which was not an easy task, in fact beyond Nehemiah's capacity. When the purpose is genuine, honest and unselfish, a leader can influence whether master or boss or servant or colleague in an organization.

Leadership is a relationship of influence.

People today look for a leader whom they can trust and influence them with a character of integrity. John Maxwell recommends following positive characters of an influencing leader.[1]

- *Model consistency of character*
- *Employ honest communication*
- *Value transparency*
- *Exemplify humility*

> "The key to successful leadership today is influence, not authority"
>
> **Kenneth Blanchard**

- *Demonstrate your support of others*
- *Fulfill your promises*

Leadership can influence positively and/or negatively. Negative influence comes normally from power and position. People remember positive influence more than negative. In history, we can see leaders with great influencing power like Hitler, who could influence as wished. People hardly remember such leaders because of their negative attitude or influence, which did not help people. We also see leaders who had tremendous positive influence on the people and world. One can think of Mahatma Gandhi, Abraham Lincoln and Martin Luther. Even today, no one questions his or her leadership qualities.

> Among leaders who lack insight, abuse abounds, but for one who hates corruption, the future is bright (Proverbs 18:16)

A good leader is not only important but also essential, without leaders neither church nor any organization including nation can prosper. If nation has good leader, it will prosper and bad leader can be doomed. This is true with our churches, family and community.

A leader has to be a great influencer and stabilizer and negotiator. Good leaders tend to be relatively stable over a period of years. While poor leaders periodically strike off in radically different directions. Good leaders commonly stick with their handful of central values and convictions. Innovation takes the form of finding new and different ways to achieve old goals that have not changed in decades of the leader's life. Another common form of instability is quitting. Unstable leaders leave the work for various reasons, while good leaders are present and accounted for year in and year out. Many, who demonstrate terrific natural charismatic leadership ability, end up being poor leaders because of the erratic course of their lives, while others who manifest little natural leadership end up being respected and effective leaders, because of their sheer dogged focus on basic spiritual principles. In times of crises, people tend to fall apart and panic, often proposing destructive radical solutions to the problems at hand. A good leader is the one who stands firm under crises and cannot be moved from the foundation of truth. People are attracted to such stability and reliability, rightly discerning that such reliability is the result of clear vision for God's way.

Uzziah king of Judah was sixteen years old when he became king, and he ruled Jerusalem fifty-two years. He did what was right in the eyes of the Lord, just as his father Amaziah had done. He sought God during the days of Zechariah, who instructed him in the fear of God. As long as he sought the Lord, God gave him success and could stabilize his kingdom. (2 Chronicles 26)

Every leader will have a character of conviction. Conviction implies leader's personal conduct. Conviction can be described as "holding a value or belief so firmly that it influences attitudes or action". Conviction inspires; faith, confidence, optimism, enthusiasm and persuasiveness.

If you cannot communicate, you cannot lead people.

Chapter 21

A Communicator and Passion Infuser

A leader has to be a good communicator, willing to listen and talk, give information. Oratory is an important tool in the treasury of a leader. As a leader, communication skills set the tone for interaction among the people. More than leader's message, how it is communicated is important. Followers listen and follow the leader, when the message is clear and has a purpose. Communication skills also involve leaders' power to convince or creating passion towards the purpose and organization. If you cannot communicate, you cannot lead people. Leaders need to learn to be proficient in both the communication that informs and seeks out information and the communication that connects interpersonally with others. Communication is another example of leadership skill that must be cultivated by all leaders.

People of Israelites followed King Samuel because he had qualities as a good communicator – simplified the message, he knew the audience or listener, he demonstrated credibility with passion and truth, and he had strong purpose in his message.

Paul's sermon recorded in Acts 17 is a masterpiece. Paul connected brilliantly with people. Note how Paul as a master communicator connected with his followers: he began with affirmation, he was familiar with his subjects, he enlarged vision of God, he used inclusive language, he encouraged and gave hope, and he gave specific action steps. Communication skill also includes consistency, clarity and courteous. Do not forget as a leader, your communication sets the tone for the interaction among people[1].

John W. Gardner[2] observed, "If I had to name of single all-purpose instrument of leadership, it would be communication. If you cannot communicate, you will not lead others effectively."

A leader can be successful if he is an effective communicator. John Maxwell suggests four truths for effective leader: simplify your message, see the person, show the truth, and seek a response.

Churchill was a great master communicator and won the people's feeling and support. His memorial expression still people remember: "I have nothing to offer but blood, toil, sweat and tears."[3]

Leaders may often suggest nothing new or different from what people are already doing, but leaders bring a sense of urgency, excitement, or passion to those activities. Leaders' own passion becomes contagious. People are drawn to passionate, excited people as they seek passion and excitement in their own lives. If we learn how to get passion and excitement in our own minds regarding the things of God, leadership is sure to show, and people will be influenced as a result.

Leaders have to speak to transform not merely inform. Passion infuser needs technical skills to change and have better understanding of the attitude and motivational demands of their followers.

Moses and Joshua attracted people because they were passionate and excited in their own life. These two leaders communicated not only with words but through their conduct, gesture and confidence.

Jesus spoke parables; Sermon on Mount is a masterpiece of communication. Jesus gave two injunctions; "Love the Lord with all thy heart, with thy mind and with all thy soul. Love thy neighbor as thyself". This kind of communication not only touches heart, the but is worth remembering. Therefore, Jesus is a master teacher.

If you lead your team, give yourself three standards to live by as you communicate to your people[4]

1. Be consistent. Nothing frustrates team members more than leaders who cannot make up their minds

2. Be clear. Your team cannot excuse you if they don't know what you want. Don't try to dazzle anyone with your intelligence; impress them with your simple straight forwardness

3. Be courteous. Everyone deserves to be shown respect, no matter what his or her position or what kind of history you might have with him or her. If you are courteous to your people, you set a tone for the entire organization.

A man can give without loving,
but he can never love without giving.

Chapter 22

A Loving and Compassionate Heart

The light of a whole life dies
when love is gone.

F.W. Bourdillon

L ove is a strong positive emotion of regard and affection. Compassion means the humane quality of understanding the suffering of others and wanting to do something about it. Lala[1], believes, compassion is deep feeling for and understanding of misery or suffering and the concomitant/ associated desire to promote its alleviation. Compassion is different from pity. Pity suggests condescension (an attitude of patronizing superiority). Compassion connotes a greater dignity in the object of attention accompanied by an urgent desire to aid.

A leader who has love and compassion will have character of generosity. Every Christian leader needs to be generous with his/ her time and financial resources. A man or woman can give without loving, but he or she can never love without giving.

"For God so loved the world that he gave his one and only Son, that whoever believes in him shall not perish but have eternal life" (John 3:16).

A Christian leader must set an example through giving, so that everyone in his/her organization follows him/her. Generosity is an expression of love of God. A leader, who is in love with God, will give his/her time and money to his/her people. Generosity includes, love and compassion.

Joseph forgives his brothers and loved them with gifts and food. He not only saved his people but all of Egypt from starvation. Where there is forgiveness, one can see love and care as a leader.

King David expressed his love and concern, even when he was fleeing from Absalom's conspiracy. The king said to Ittai the Gittite, "Why should you come along with us? Go back and stay with king Absalom. And today shall I make you wander about with us, when I do not know where I am going? Go back and take your countrymen. May kindness and faithfulness be with you?" Ittai replied to the king, "As surely as the Lord lives, and as my lord the king lives, wherever my lord the king may be, whether it means life or death, there will your servant be."

What are the lessons? David was kind, sympathetic, loving and caring, even during his troubles. Ittai, was sincere to his master, He could have left the king but he chose to be with him by risking his life and future (2 Samuel 15:19-21).

Nehemiah helps the poor when there was an outcry among his people (Nehemiah 5).

Boaz was kind with his workers and showed compassion to the poor Ruth. A good leader is compassionate to those in need. (Ruth 2).

But the Lord said to Samuel,

"Do not look at his appearance or at his physical stature, because I
have refused him. For the Lord does not see as man sees, for man
looks at the outward appearance but the Lord looks at the heart"
(1 Samuel 16:7).

God chose David to be king of Israelites because God saw his
compassionate heart and tenderness in spirit. David was a warrior
but was very gentle. David started his leadership with humility,
faithfulness, responsibility, and loves for God and committed his
heart for God. Today's leaders need to emulate David as they climb
the ladder of leadership.

When Jerusalem fell to King Nebuchadnezzar in 587 BC, the
Babylonians burnt down the royal palace and Nebuchadnezzar had
the King of Judah blinded. Almost fifty years later Cyrus, founder
of the Persian Empire, is believed to have received a revelation
from the Lord of

Israel; "to rebuild my city Jerusalem and set my people free"
When Cyrus conquered Babylon he liberated the Jews and directed
them to go and rebuild Jerusalem. In the Age of religious intolerance,
Cyrus demonstrated remarkable tolerance; in an age of cruelty he
showed magnanimity as well as concern.[2]

Endnotes

Chapter 1

[1] John Zechariah, Youth Capacity Building-Spiritual and Responsible Leadership Formation, Manila, Philippines, 2008.

[2] J. Oswald Sanders, Spiritual Leadership, Authentic Books, 1994, p.29.

Chapter 2

[1] John Maxwell, Leadership, Promises For Every Day, Maxwell Motivation, Inc, 2003, p.203.

Discipline	Application
Abstinence from wine/strong drinks prevent addiction	Self-control: discipline to
Uncut hair	Image: refuse to allow fashion to lead you.
Avoid defilement from corpse	Integrity: stay pure; pursue and a holy standard

[2] D. Quinn Mills, Leadership: How to Lead, How to Live, Waltham, MA; MindEdge Press, 2003.

[3] John Maxwell, 2005, p.334.

Chapter 3

[1] Hayford's Bible Handbook, p.570.

[2] Michael Houdmann, What is Christian leadership? got. Question?.org

[3] Ricky Farley, Attitudes of great Leaders, Authentic Books, Hyderabad, 2006.

[4] John MacArthur, "wanted": A few Good Shepherds. As quoted by Michael Houdmann, What is Christian leadership?

Chapter 4

[1] D. Quinn Mills, Leadership: How to Lead, How to Live, Waltham, MA; MindEdge Press, 2005.

[2] John Maxwell, Leadership, Promises For Every Day, Maxwell Motivation Inc, 2003, p.9.

[3] Azim Premji.

[4] Importance of Leadership, *managementstudyguide.com*.

Chapter 5

[1] Number 4-6, as mentioned in article Gladiators for God.

[2] Number 7-9 as mentioned in article, Wikipedia, the free encyclopedia.

[3] R.M. Lala, In Search of Ethical Leadership, Vision Books, Delhi, 2005, p.19.

[4] Stephen L. Cohen, Engaging Style, for leading organization in touch times, as mentioned in article Wikipedia, the free encyclopedia.

Chapter 6

[1] Christian Leadership, The Principles of good Christian leadership, Gladiators for God.

[2] General Douglas McArthur, Douglas Quotes, *www.bing.com*.

[3] John Maxwell, Leadership, Promises for Every Day, Maxwell Motivation, Inc, 2005, p.96.

[4] John Maxwell, Leadership, Promises for Every Day, p.184.

[5] Dave Quinn, Principles of Christian Leadership, Passion Australia, *www.passionaustralia.org*.

Chapter 7

[1] John Zechariah, Leadership Formation, at Association Christian Institutes of Social Concern in Asia (ACISCA) Christian Lay Leadership Training, at Kottayam, India, 2007.

[2] Omker Phatak, Leadership Development Plan, *www.buzzle.com*, 2011, quoted in Leadership, Christian Methodist Episcopal, Department of Christian Education.

Chapter 8

[1] The paper presented by John Zechariah at ACISCA's CCLT training at Kottayam, India, 2007.

[2] Ryan C. Nelsen, Leadership: Qualification of a Leader, *Youth Pasor.com*, 1997.

Chapter 9

[1] John Zechariah, Youth Capacity Building-Spiritual and Responsible Leadership Formation, Manila, Philippines, 2008.

[2] John Zechariah, Empowering Youth to Empower Asia in the 21st Century, Opening Address, Christian Lay Leadership Training (CCLT), at MBM, Bali, Indonesia, 2009.

[3] John Zechariah, International Enrichment Training for Christian Youth Leadership in Asia, ACISCA, Bangkok, Thailand, November 2012.

[4] Read John Maxwell, Leadership, Promises for Every Day, p.223.

[5] Bernard Grant, First Class Leaders, Milestone International Publishers, USA, 2004, p.31.

Chapter 10

[1] As mentioned by John Maxwell, Leadership, Promises For Every Day, p.49.

[2] John Maxwell, Leadership, Promises For Every Day, p.151.

Chapter 11

[1] Read John Maxwell, Leadership, Promise For Every Day, p.206.

[2] John Maxwell, Leadership, Promise For Every Day, p.232.

[3] Mike Murdock - The Leadership Secrets of Jesus, p.70.

[4] Read John Maxwell, Leadership, Promise For Every Day, p.276.

[5] Read John Maxwell, Leadership, Promise For Every Day, p.153.

[6] Malcolm Webber, Building Leaders, SpiritBuilt Leadership 4, pp.99-109.

Chapter 13

John Maxwell, Leadership, Promises for Every Day, p.79.

John Maxwell, Leadership, Promises for Every Day, p.213.

Chapter 14

[1] Lala, In Search of Ethical Leadership, pp.59-60.

[2] John Maxwell, Leadership, Promises of Every Day, p.72.

[3] Andy Stanley, The Next Generation Leader, Authentic Headlines, 2003, p.58.

Chapter 15

[1] John Maxwell, Leadership, Promises for Every Day, p.212.

Chapter 16

[1] Dennis McCallum, What is Christian Leader? 12 Ways to Conceive of Leaders, Xenos Christian Fellowship, 2012.

[2] What should we learn from the account of David and Goliath? gotQuestions?org

Chapter 18

[1] John Maxwell, Leadership, Promises For Every Day, p.16.

Chapter 20

[1] John Maxwell, Leadership, Promise For Every Day.

Chapter 21

[1] John Maxwell, Leadership, for Every Day, pp.332, 92.

[2] John W. Gardner, as mentioned by John Maxwell, p.192.

[3] R.M Lala, In Search of Ethical Leadership, p.25.

[4] John Maxwell, Leadership, for Every Day, p.192.

www.ingramcontent.com/pod-product-compliance
Lightning Source LLC
Chambersburg PA
CBHW060833250626
47162CB00005B/2046